Half-Baked Gourmet

PARTLY HOMEMADE TOTALLY DELICIOUS

PASTA

*200 Quick-and-Easy Recipes
for Every Occasion*

Jean Galton

A ROUNDTABLE PRESS BOOK

HPBOOKS

D0101154

Notice: The recipes in this book are to be followed exactly as written. Neither the publisher nor the author is responsible for your specific health or allergy needs that may require medical supervision, or for any adverse reactions to the recipes contained in this book.

HPBooks
Published by The Berkley Publishing Group
A division of Penguin Group (USA) Inc.
375 Hudson Street
New York, New York 10014

Copyright © 2005 Roundtable Press, Inc.
Design: Charles Kreloff
Illustrations: Tony Persiani
Cover photograph © Foodpix/David Roth

www.roundtablepressinc.com
For Roundtable Press, Inc.:
Directors: Julie Merberg, Marsha Melnick
Executive Editor: Patty Brown
Editor: Sara Newberry

First edition: February 2005

This book has been cataloged with the Library of Congress.
ISBN 1-55788-442-0
Printed and bound in China
10 9 8 7 6 5 4 3 2 1

Contents

Pasta is the original healthy, low-fat, great-tasting food. Throw it into boiling water and in less than 10 minutes, it's cooked. Toss it with a sauce and dinner is ready. And that's what **The Half-Baked Gourmet: Pasta** is all about. In this book you'll find dozens of flavorful and fast pasta recipes from everyday dinners and simple, no-stress pastas perfect for company to fast brunches and quick lunches. The recipes in this book require little chopping, few pots and pans, and the most basic cooking know-how. Each recipe uses a pared-down list of ingredients featuring the best-quality prepared foods, so your efforts will be on the table, ready to eat, in no time flat. Your pasta dishes will burst with flavor and you'll be feeding your family great-tasting, healthy food.

A WORD ON INGREDIENTS

Since many of the recipes in this book contain just a handful of ingredients, it's crucial that the ingredients you buy are the freshest and finest you can afford. Each item, from the butter to the pasta to the salt to the tomatoes, must be flavorful or the dish simply won't be at its best. When possible, I choose foods that contain all-natural ingredients and organic over nonorganic. I also try to avoid foods containing nitrites, hydrogenated oils, corn syrup, and preservatives.

A WORD ON CARBOHYDRATES

In recent years, carbohydrates have gotten a bad rap. Several popular high-protein diets are built around avoiding carbohydrates, including pasta, on the premise that they make people gain weight. Pasta, in and of itself, does not cause weight gain. Burning fewer calories than your body takes in is what usually leads to weight gain. Pasta is particularly rich in glutamic acid, a brain-enhancing amino acid. It also contains thiamin (Vitamin B_1), an important vitamin that regulates carbohydrate metabolism. Once in the body, pasta breaks down into glucose, or pure energy, which is why many marathoners and cyclists eat large spaghetti dinners the night before a race. And pasta is an integral part of the healthy Mediterranean diet—along with healthy oils (such as olive oil), lots of vegetables and fruit, small amounts of meat, fish, and poultry, and multi-grained bread.

PASTA

There are many brands of dried pastas on the market, both mass-produced and artisanal. Since artisanal pastas cost a little more, I tend to save them for entertaining rather than for everyday. For everyday pastas, I like Barilla, a widely available Italian import. I also like DeCecco and Delverde, both imported brands with a mild wheat flavor.

Artisanal pastas are extruded through rough dies and dried slowly. This produces a lovely roughly textured surface (which makes sauces cling better) with a well-developed, nutty flavor. My favorite is made by an Italian company, Rustichella d'Abruzzo.

Fresh pasta is found in the refrigerated section of the supermarket. Other than a few small fresh pasta makers such as Rising Moon Organics, however, I have found most supermarket brands to be flavorless and tough. I recommend finding a local pasta company from whom to buy fresh pasta.

OILS

In many of the recipes in this book, I cook with **extra-virgin olive oil**. The best extra-virgin olive oils are new, cold-pressed oils, either from Italy, Spain, or California, and all are very flavorful and, equally, quite expensive. I usually reserve these for drizzling onto recipes at the end of cooking or for salads. For everyday use, I usually cook with a slightly less expensive product, such as Puglia Extra-Virgin Olive Oil or Napoleon Organic Extra-Virgin Olive Oil. Extra-virgin olive oil gives dishes a particular flavor, so it's best not to substitute oils like light olive oil or corn oil where extra-virgin olive oil is specified. Flavored oils such as Consorzio Basil-Flavored Olive Oil or Pacifica Culinaria Lemon-Flavored Avocado Oil add subtle flavor without any extra effort. Look for these in the specialty foods section or in gourmet shops.

TOMATOES AND TOMATO SAUCES

The best brands of **canned tomatoes** have a sweet tomato flavor and cook up into bright, fresh sauces in minutes. Muir Glen and Trader Joe's are the best organic canned tomatoes I've found. They're available whole, diced, ground, and fire-roasted with or without green chiles. Among nonorganic brands, I like Redpack and San Marzano.

Peruse the pasta sauce shelves and you'll find some excellent choices. Barilla and Muir Glen both make very flavorful marinara sauces, while Mario Batali's Tomato Sauce is a good all-purpose sauce. If you're choosing a tomato sauce and don't know which to pick, choose one with the natural ingredients. For a pick-me-up to the cooked flavor of jarred sauces, I mix in a cup or so of canned diced tomatoes for a much brighter taste.

BROTHS

I prefer to buy **aseptic containers** of chicken, vegetable, and beef broths rather than cans. Broths from these containers have a fresher taste and come in handy 1-cup and 1-quart sizes. The broth stays fresh after opening for about a week in the fridge. If I don't think I'll be using what's left over in time, I freeze the remainder in another container.

GARLIC

Chopped and peeled garlic are available jarred (Christopher Ranch has garlic without additives). While this will save you time, the flavor doesn't compare with freshly chopped garlic. It takes a little time to learn to mince garlic properly, but once you've mastered it, it only takes a minute. In these recipes, I've specified the amounts of garlic in measurements so you can use jarred garlic, if you prefer. Buy the smallest jar you can find, and don't keep it longer than a couple of weeks.

CHEESE

Parmigiana Reggiano and pecorino Romano are both Italian cheeses I call for in this book. The best are imported from Italy. You can usually find them already shredded or grated. Mozzarella, Asiago, and Cheddar, all available shredded as well. **Blue cheese, goat cheese, and feta crumbles** can be found in the cheese section and are perfect for sprinkling over pasta and in salads too. **Herbed**

cheeses such as Boursin or Alouette bring intense flavor to pasta dishes and can be tossed with hot pasta for an instant cheese sauce. **Mascarpone** is an Italian cream cheese that adds luxurious richness to pasta sauces. And **ricotta**, a moist and mildly flavored cheese, is always available in the dairy section. I buy the whole milk or part-skim varieties, not the nonfat. **Fresh ricotta** has a more delicate taste and texture than packaged. If your supermarket has it, try it—you'll notice a difference.

BUTTER

I use **unsalted butter**, because I prefer to control the salt in recipes and salted butters vary greatly in saltiness. Quality among brands also varies, with lower-cost butters containing more water. For a standard nonorganic butter, I like unsalted Land O'Lakes. As far as organic butter, I have found that Trader Joe's Organic Butter has good flavor and costs less than many nonorganic butters. Horizon and Organic Valley are also excellent organic brands. For special occasions, I like to use European-style butters, such as Plugra or Lurpak. They're higher in fat than American-style butter and fabulous in pasta dishes.

SALT

Salt is an integral part of cooking pasta. I use **coarse kosher salt** and I like Diamond Crystal Kosher Salt. The other kosher salt on the market is Morton's, which has a more intense, concentrated salt flavor. If you use Morton's kosher salt, you'll need to use less salt than Diamond Crystal. If I use fine salt, I use a natural sea salt such as Baleine.

HERBS

I use lots of fresh herbs when I cook pasta, especially flat-leaf Italian parsley and basil. When purchasing fresh herbs, look for brightly colored, unblemished leaves. Herbs such as parsley, cilantro, basil, and mint last beautifully with their stems placed in a glass of water. Cover the leaves with a plastic bag, tuck the bottom of the bag into the glass, and refrigerate.

Dried herbs are easier to keep on hand than fresh, and I have used them in many of the recipes for this book. The key to flavorful dried herbs is storage: keep them in a cool, dark place (not over the stove) and keep them only for about a year.

FRESH VEGETABLES AND GREENS

Bags of washed salad greens and spinach are some of the best time-saving products around—you just open the bag and you're ready to go. There are many different mixes and varieties available. For the freshest greens, always check the sell-by date. I buy organic salad greens—Earthbound Farms offers consistently fresh organic mixes.

Precut vegetables also save lots of time. I use precut cauliflower and broccoli florets and presliced mushrooms in many of the recipes in this book.

CITRUS

Citrus juice and zest add big flavor with little effort. Shop for organic citrus fruit with taut, shiny skins, and make sure they're heavy with juice. If the fruit feels heavy for its size, odds are it's very juicy.

FISH

With the advent of increasingly more sophisticated freezing methods, fine-quality frozen fish is much more widely available than ever before. Much of the frozen fish sold in supermarkets has been flash-frozen at sea and retains its fresh flavor. Supermarkets sometimes sell **individually quick-frozen (IQF) seafood** such as scallops, crab legs, lobster tails, squid, and shrimp from bins near the fish counter, so you can keep some on hand in your freezer. IQF fish is much easier to use than traditional blocks of frozen fish: just put the fish or shellfish in cold water and it thaws in minutes.

When shopping for fresh fish, look for shiny, moist flesh and don't hesitate to ask to smell it. Fresh fish smells faintly of the ocean. If it has a strong odor, it's not fresh, so don't buy it.

MEATS AND POULTRY

When shopping for fresh meat and poultry, I always opt for **organic free-range, grass-fed and finished meats,** which are fed on grass for their entire lives. These products have been raised with care and, as a result, have a much better flavor and texture. Niman Ranch meats, Diestal Turkey products, and Rosie chickens are a few brands that I like.

For cooked and smoked meats and poultry, I like the Applegate Farms brand of uncured salami, smoked turkey, and Black Forest ham. These are available sliced to order at the supermarket deli counter. Niman Ranch also makes a fine Black Forest ham, although you'll need to slice it yourself.

WINE

Never use cooking wine in your food. The rule of thumb for cooking with wine is to use a wine that's good enough to drink. Inexpensive good-quality wines produced by winemakers such as Yellowtail, Hogue, Woodbridge, and Columbia Crest are good to keep on hand for cooking (or to offer to surprise visitors). Any of the wines from these cellars will work when deglazing a pan or adding to a sauce. If you'd prefer to avoid alcohol, just substitute the same amount of broth for the wine.

PASTA TECHNIQUES

Boil, Salt, and Stir!

The key to the best flavor from pasta is cooking it properly. If you're cooking a pound of pasta, use a large saucepot (having enough room in the pot helps keep pasta from sticking together) and 4 to 5 quarts of water. For less pasta, 2 quarts should do.

Before adding the pasta, let the water boil first, then add salt. I usually use coarse kosher salt, and I add 3 to 4 tablespoons per 4 to 5 quarts of water. If I use fine salt, I use 1 to 2 tablespoons. Without salt, pasta is quite bland. Salting the water properly also helps season the final dish.

As soon as you've added the salt, add the pasta and stir. When pasta hits boiling water it starts to release starch, which can make the it stick together. Stirring for the first minute or so can prevent the pasta from becoming glued together.

No Oil

Many people add oil to the cooking water. I don't, because while this does help to keep the water from boiling over, it can make the pasta oily and prevent the sauce from being absorbed. If you're worried about the pot boiling over, reduce the heat slightly.

Save the Pasta Water

Before you drain the pasta, save some of the cooking water. The cooking water has starch dissolved into it and adding a few tablespoons to your sauce will enrich its texture, as well as help it to thicken.

Taste It

Most pasta should be cooked al dente, or "to the tooth." Use the cooking times given in the recipes or on the package as guidelines, but the only reliable way test pastafor doneness is to taste it. If it's no longer chalky inside but has a little resistance when you bite into it, it's done. If it's mushy, it's overcooked.

Rice noodles, somen, and soba should be cooked all the way through. Again, the most reliable way to test it is to taste it. As soon as the noodles are cooked to your taste, drain them.

Keep It Hot

The hotter the pasta, the more flavor it will absorb from the sauce, so if you're serving the pasta directly from stove to table, it's usually best to go straight from draining to mixing. Cold salads, baked pastas, and specialty noodles (such as soba or rice noodles) are exceptions to this rule.

EQUIPMENT

You'll need a saucepot large enough to hold 4 to 6 quarts of water. You'll also need a colander large enough to hold a pound of cooked pasta, so you won't run the risk of the hot pasta overflowing and spilling out into the sink.

If you're cooking pasta several times a week, I recommend buying a pasta pot with a colander fitted to it. When the pasta is ready, you simply lift out the colander with the pasta, leaving the hot water behind.

Another essential piece of equipment is a 12-inch skillet, which I use to make quick tomato sauces. Since the skillet is so wide, there's more opportunity for surface evaporation to occur, so sauces thicken and flavors concentrate very quickly. You'll also find recipes in this book where pastas are finished in the sauce—it's much easier to use a wide skillet than the pasta pot. I have two skillets that I use nearly every day: a stainless steel, heavy-bottomed 12-inch skillet and a nonstick 12-inch skillet.

You'll also need a few long-handled wooden spoons. I especially like the ones made from hardwood with pointed asymmetrical tips, which are great for stirring sauces. An inexpensive pair of 12-inch tongs make serving up spaghetti and noodles effortless. You'll need a sharp 8- or 10-inch chef's knife, a small, sharp paring knife, and a sharp vegetable peeler. If your peeler is more than a few years old, it's time to buy a new one with a sharp blade. I couldn't cook without my microplane to grate lemon, lime, and orange zest. And a food processor for fast chopping and puréeing will perfectly complete your pasta kitchen.

FREEZER, FRIDGE AND PANTRY

Following is a list of the ingredients I call for in the recipes in this book. Keep your favorites on hand (for your favorite recipes) and you'll always be ready to serve up something tasty. All that's missing are the occasional fresh ingredients: fruits, vegetables, herbs, and fresh meats.

IN THE FREEZER...

VEGETABLES
Cascadian Farms® shelled
  edamame
Cascadian Farms® corn
Cascadian Farms® peas
Cascadian Farms® broccoli
Cascadian Farms® cauliflower
Stahlbush Island Farms organic
  sweet potatoes
Stahlbush Island Farms organic
  butternut squash
Stahlbush Island Farms organic
  peas
Stahlbush Island Farms organic
  string beans
C & W pepper strips
C & W petite peas
C & W haricot vert
Baby white corn
Cauliflower
Mustard greens
Baby lima beans
Whole leaf spinach
Chopped spinach

FISH AND SHELLFISH
Shelled and deveined shrimp
Cooked shrimp
Scallops
Squid, pre-cut
Rock lobster tails
Lump crabmeat

NUTS
Almonds
Walnuts
Pine nuts
Peanuts

IN THE FRIDGE...

DAIRY
Trader Joe's® unsalted organic
  butter
Organic Valley® unsalted
  organic butter
Land O'Lakes® unsalted butter
Smoked gouda
Smoked mozzarella
Fresh mozzarella
Feta cheese crumbles
Blue cheese crumbles
Shredded mozzarella cheese
Shredded cheddar cheese
Shredded Italian cheese blend
Shredded Mexican cheese blend
Grated Parmesan cheese
Grated pecorino Romano cheese
Grated Asiago cheese
Mediterra feta in oil with herbs
  and spices
Boursin® herb and garlic cheese
Boursin® black pepper cheese
Alta Dena® crème fraîche
Bellwether Farms crème fraîche
Organic Valley® cream cheese
Laura Chenel goat cheese

Ricotta cheese
Ricotta salata
Mascarpone
Milk
Organic Valley heavy cream
Plain yogurt
Total® Greek yogurt
Queso fresco

SAUCES AND CONDIMENTS
Cibo Naturals™ Classic basil pesto
Cibo Naturals™ sun-dried
  tomato pesto
Cibo Naturals™ tapenade
Salsa

SMOKED AND CURED MEATS
Applegate Farms® smoked turkey
Applegate® Farms Black Forest
  ham
Applegate Farms® Sunday
  bacon
Prosciutto
Pancetta
Niman Ranch Black Forest ham
Thick Cut bacon
Hillshire Farms® kielbasa
Chorizo
Pepperoni
Andouille sausage

SEAFOOD
Lox

MISCELLANEOUS ITEMS
Pitted Kalamata olives
Pitted Sicilian green olives
Niçoise olives
Christopher Ranch® chopped garlic
Christopher Ranch® ginger
Baked tofu
Extra-firm tofu
Western Family® evaporated milk

IN THE PANTRY...

PASTA
Everyday pastas
Barilla®
Ronzoni®
DeCecco®
Colavita®
Delverde®
Mueller's® egg noodles
Rosetto® Cheese Ravioli
Rosetto® Tortellini
Rising Moon® Mushroom Ravioli
Trader Joe's® Dried Tortellini
Couscous

Artisanal pastas
Rustichella d'Abruzzo®
Gerardo Di Nola®
Latini®
Emilia® Gnocchi

TOMATOES AND TOMATO SAUCES
Muir Glen® Whole Peeled Italian Tomatoes
Muir Glen® Diced Italian Tomatoes
Muir Glen® Ground Peeled Tomatoes
Muir Glen® Fire-Roasted Tomatoes
Muir Glen® Diced Fire-Roasted Tomatoes
Muir Glen® Fire-Roasted Whole Tomatoes with Chiles
Red Pack® Whole Peeled Tomatoes
Trader Joe's® Diced Organic Peeled Tomatoes
Barilla® Marinara Sauce
Barilla® Tomato Sauce
Trader Joe's® Tomato Sauce
Trader Joe's® Organic Tomato Sauce
Muir Glen® Fire Roasted Tomato Sauce
Muir Glen® Cabernet Marinara Sauce
Mario Batali® Basic Tomato Sauce
Newman's Own® Tomato Sauce

VINEGARS AND OILS
Spectrum Naturals® peanut oil
Spectrum Naturals® canola oil
Spectrum Naturals® olive oil
Napoleon® extra-virgin olive oil
Puglia® extra-virgin olive oil
Trader Giotto's® extra-virgin olive oil
Trader Joe's® garlic-flavored olive oil
Consorzio® lemon-flavored olive oil
Consorzio® orange-flavored olive oil
Consorzio® basil-flavored olive oil
Pacificia Culinaria™ Coastal lemon-flavored avocado oil
Shirakiku sesame oil
Eden hot pepper sesame oil
Spectrum Naturals® red wine vinegar
Cider vinegar
365™ balsamic vinegar
Napoleon organic balsamic vinegar
Mitsukan rice vinegar

SALAD DRESSINGS, SAUCES, AND CONDIMENTS
(refrigerate after opening)
Annie's Naturals® sesame and ginger vinaigrette
Annie's Naturals® shiitake and sesame vinaigrette
Newman's Own® Caesar dressing
Newman's Own® balsamic dressing
Newman's Own® olive oil and vinegar dressing
S & B® prepared wasabi paste
Sun Luck pickled sliced ginger
Sun Luck spicy oyster sauce

Kikkoman Lite Soy Sauce
Kikkoman Teriyaki Sauce and
    Marinade
Lee Kum Kee Black Bean Sauce
Huy Fong sriracha sauce
Thai Kitchen rice noodles
Thai Kitchen coconut milk
Thai Kitchen® green curry paste
Thai Kitchen® roasted chile paste
Thai Kitchen® fish sauce
Chaokoh coconut milk
Three Crabs fish sauce
Muir Glen® organic ketchup
Heinz® organic ketchup
Harissa
Hellman's® mayonnaise
Grey Poupon® Dijon mustard
Trader Joe's® Sun-dried Tomato
    Pesto
Napoleon Anchovy Paste
Muir Glen® Chipotle Salsa

VEGETABLES
(refrigerate after opening)
Westbrae Natural® chickpeas
Walnut Acres® lentils
Progresso® cannelini beans
Starkist® white tuna in olive oil
Trader Joe's® white tuna in
    olive oil
Trader Joe's® Red Salmon
Trader Joe's® Smoked Alaskan
    Salmon
King Oscar brisling sardines
Snows® chopped clams
Crown Prince® crabmeat
Napoleon anchovies

Napoleon capers
Napoleon marinated
    mushrooms
Napoleon baby corn
Napoleon marinated spicy
    artichoke hearts
Trader Joe's® marinated
    artichoke hearts
Trader Joe's® roasted peppers
Talatta anchovies
Trader Joe's® sun-dried
    tomatoes in oil
Trader Joe's® Roasted Peppers
    with Garlic
Krinos® Roasted Peppers
La Morena® chipotles in adobo

BROTHS
(refrigerate after opening)
Pacific Foods® vegetable broth
Pacific Foods® beef broth
Pacific Foods® free range
    chicken broth
Pacific Foods® organic low-
    sodium chicken broth
Swanson® low-sodium chicken
    broth

SPICE SHELF AND DRY GOODS
Diamond Crystal® kosher salt
Morton's® kosher salt
Baleine® sea salt
Tellicherry peppercorns
Bay leaves
Turmeric
Star anise
Saffron

Cinnamon
Mint
Marjoram
Oregano
Nutmeg
Fennel seed
Paprika
Ginger
Cayenne
Herbes de provence
Cumin
Coriander
Red pepper flakes
Madras curry powder
Sugar
Light brown sugar
Toasted sesame seeds
Honey
Dried porcini mushrooms
Dried currants
Cornstarch

WINE AND LIQUOR
White wine
Red wine
Sherry
Marsala

Baked, Stuffed, and Filled Pasta

Manicotti with Spinach Ricotta Stuffing

For a change of pace, sprinkle the top of the manicotti with shredded fontina.

PREP TIME: 20 MINUTES • COOK TIME: 25 MINUTES • MAKES: 6 SERVINGS

3 tablespoons unsalted butter

1 medium yellow onion, chopped

Pinch red pepper flakes

1 package (10 ounces) frozen chopped
   spinach, thawed and drained

1 1/2 cups ricotta cheese

1 cup grated pecorino Romano cheese

1/4 teaspoon grated nutmeg

Salt and freshly ground black pepper

Olive oil pan spray

1 package (13 ounces, about 12 noodles)
   fresh lasagna noodles

1 cup heavy cream

1 can (15 ounces) tomato sauce

1 1/2 cups canned diced tomatoes

1 1/2 cups shredded mozzarella cheese

1. Heat the oven to 500°F. In a large skillet over medium-high heat, melt the butter.

Add the onion and cook until soft, 3 to 4 minutes. Add the pepper flakes and spinach and cook, stirring frequently, until spinach is heated through, about 3 minutes. Transfer to a medium bowl and stir in the ricotta, pecorino, and nutmeg. Season generously with salt and pepper.

2. Spray a 13 x 9-inch baking dish with the olive oil spray. Lay a lasagna noodle on a work surface and spoon 1/4 cup of the filling in the middle; roll up. Place in the prepared baking dish and continue rolling and filling the noodles until you have used all of the filling.

3. In another bowl, stir together the cream, tomato sauce, and tomatoes. Pour over the filled noodles. Sprinkle with the mozzarella and bake until browned and bubbling around the edges, 10 to 15 minutes.

Quattro Formaggio Lasagna

A great dish for entertaining, this delicious lasagna can be made and refrigerated up to a day ahead of time. Freeze (before baking) for up to a month. If you do choose to freeze it, thaw in the fridge before baking.

PREP TIME: 35 MINUTES • COOK TIME: 35 MINUTES • MAKES: 6 SERVINGS

4 tablespoons unsalted butter
3 tablespoons all-purpose flour
2¼ cups milk
Salt and freshly ground black pepper
Pinch cayenne pepper
1 container (15 ounces) ricotta cheese
1½ cups shredded smoked Gouda or
    smoked mozzarella cheese
1 package (12 ounces) shredded
    mozzarella cheese
1 cup grated Parmesan cheese
½ pound instant lasagna noodles

1. Heat the oven to 375°F. In a medium saucepan over medium-high heat, melt 3 tablespoons butter. Whisk in the flour and simmer until golden, about 2 minutes. Remove the pan from the heat and gradually whisk in the milk until smooth. Return to the heat, bring to boiling, and season with salt, black pepper, and cayenne pepper. Simmer until thickened and smooth, about 3 minutes. Whisk in the ricotta and set aside. In a medium bowl, mix together the remaining three cheeses.

2. Place the remaining butter in a 13 x 9-inch baking pan and put the pan in the oven until butter melts, about 2 minutes. Tilt pan to coat the bottom and sides. Cover with a layer of noodles. Spread with one third of the ricotta mixture and one third of the cheese. Repeat with a layer of noodles and one third of the cheese. Top with the remaining noodles, ricotta mixture, and cheese. Cover with foil and bake until bubbling around the edges and hot in the center, 30 to 35 minutes. Let stand, covered, 5 minutes before serving.

Spinach Lasagna

You won't miss the meat sauce in this cheese-filled vegetarian lasagna.

PREP TIME: 35 MINUTES • COOK TIME: 40 MINUTES • MAKES: 6 SERVINGS

6 tablespoons unsalted butter
3 tablespoons all-purpose flour
2¼ cups milk
Salt and freshly ground black pepper
Pinch cayenne pepper
1 container (15 ounces) ricotta cheese
1½ cups shredded smoked Gouda cheese
1 package (12 ounces) shredded mozzarella
   cheese
1 cup grated Parmesan cheese
1 tablespoon minced garlic
Pinch red pepper flakes
2 bags (6 to 8 ounces each) baby spinach
½ pound instant lasagna noodles

1. Heat the oven to 375°F. In a medium saucepan over medium-high heat, melt 3 tablespoons butter. Whisk in the flour and simmer until golden, about 2 minutes. Remove the pan from the heat and gradually whisk in the milk until smooth. Return to the heat, bring to boiling, and season with salt, black pepper, and cayenne pepper. Simmer until thickened, about 3 minutes. Whisk in the ricotta and set aside. In a medium bowl, mix together the remaining three cheeses.

2. In a large skillet over medium-high heat, melt 2 tablespoons of butter. Add garlic and pepper flakes. Cook 1 minute. Gradually add spinach and stir until spinach is wilted. Season with salt and black pepper.

3. Place remaining butter in a 13 x 9-inch baking pan. Put the pan in the oven until butter melts, about 2 minutes. Tilt pan to coat the bottom and sides. Cover with a layer of noodles. Spread with one third of the ricotta mixture, half the spinach, and one third of the cheese. Repeat with a layer of noodles and one third of the cheese. Top with the remaining noodles, ricotta mixture, spinach, and cheese. Cover with foil and bake until bubbling around the edges and hot in the center, 30 to 35 minutes. Let stand, covered, 5 minutes before serving.

Overstuffed Veggie Lasagna

A salad of a tender lettuce, such as bibb, and a bitter one, like radicchio, will round out the meal.

PREP TIME: 30 MINUTES • COOK TIME: 45 MINUTES • MAKES: 6 TO 8 SERVINGS

Salt
16 traditional lasagna noodles
4 tablespoons extra-virgin olive oil
4 medium carrots, peeled and thinly sliced
4 small zucchini, thinly sliced
Freshly ground black pepper
1 tablespoon minced garlic
2 teaspoons chopped fresh thyme
1 jar (25 ounces) marinara sauce
1 cup canned diced Italian tomatoes
1 package (16 ounces) frozen chopped
   spinach, thawed, moisture squeezed out
3 cups ricotta
1½ cups grated Parmesan cheese
4 cups shredded mozzarella cheese

1. Heat the oven to 375°F. In a large saucepan over high heat, bring 3 quarts water to boiling. Add salt to taste and the noodles. Cook until al dente, 6 to 8 minutes, then drain.

2. Meanwhile, in a large skillet over medium-high heat, heat 1 tablespoon oil. Add the carrots and cook, stirring, about 3 minutes. Add the zucchini, salt, and ½ cup water. Cover and cook until tender, about 3 minutes more. Season with pepper and transfer to a bowl.

3. In the same skillet over medium-high heat, heat the remaining oil. Add the garlic, thyme, marinara sauce, tomatoes, salt, and pepper and bring to simmering. Set aside.

4. In a small bowl, stir together the spinach, ricotta, and 1 cup Parmesan. Season with salt and pepper.

5. Spread ½ cup tomato sauce on the bottom of a 13 x 9-inch baking pan. Cover with a layer of noodles. Top with 1 cup sauce, 1 cup spinach mixture, 1 cup carrot mixture, and 1 cup mozzarella. Repeat twice, finishing with tomato sauce and the remaining ½ cup Parmesan. Cover pan with foil; bake 30 minutes. Uncover, sprinkle with the remaining 1 cup mozzarella and bake until bubbling and hot, 15 minutes more. Let stand 5 minutes before serving.

Artichoke and Roasted Pepper Lasagna

Pancetta adds a wonderful flavor to this lasagna, but if you prefer vegetarian lasagna, omit the pancetta and add 2 more tablespoons olive oil.

PREP TIME: 30 MINUTES • COOK TIME: 35 MINUTES • MAKES: 6 TO 8 SERVINGS

2 tablespoons extra-virgin olive oil
1 tablespoon minced garlic
Pinch red pepper flakes
4 ounces pancetta, chopped, or
   4 slices bacon
1 jar (12 ounces) marinated artichokes,
   drained and chopped
1 jar (12 ounces) roasted peppers, drained
   and chopped
1 jar (25 ounces) marinara sauce
Salt and freshly ground black pepper
1/2 pound instant lasagna noodles
8 ounces goat cheese, crumbled
3 cups shredded mozzarella cheese
1/2 cup grated Parmesan cheese

1. Heat the oven to 375°F. In a large skillet over medium-high heat, heat the oil. Add the garlic, pepper flakes, and the pancetta. Cook until the pancetta is browned, about 5 minutes. Stir in the artichokes, peppers, marinara sauce, 1/2 cup water, salt, and pepper and bring to a simmer. Remove pan from heat and set aside.

2. Cover the bottom of a 13 x 9-inch baking pan with 1/4 cup of the sauce mixture. Cover with a layer of noodles, 2 cups sauce, half of the goat cheese, and 1 cup mozzarella. Top with a layer of noodles, 2 cups sauce, the remainder of the goat cheese, and 1 cup of the mozzarella. Top with the remaining noodles, sauce, mozzarella, and Parmesan. Cover with foil and bake until bubbling and hot, 30 to 35 minutes. Let stand, covered, 5 minutes before serving.

Spinach-Tortellini Gratin

Substitute spinach tortellini or ravioli for even more spinach flavor.

PREP TIME: 5 MINUTES • COOK TIME: 20 MINUTES • MAKES: 4 SERVINGS

Salt

2 packages (9 ounces each) fresh cheese
   tortellini

4 tablespoons unsalted butter

8 ounces (½ package) frozen leaf spinach

¾ cup heavy cream

Pinch freshly grated nutmeg

Freshly ground black pepper

1 small fresh mozzarella (about 4 ounces),
   thinly sliced

½ cup grated pecorino Romano cheese

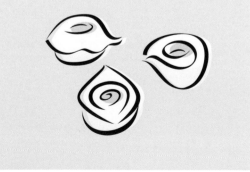

1. Heat the oven to 500°F. In a large saucepot over high heat, bring 4 quarts of water to boiling. Add salt to taste and the tortellini. Cook until just tender, about 3 minutes. Drain and transfer to an 8-inch-square baking dish.

2. In a large skillet, melt the butter over medium-high heat. Add the spinach and cook, stirring, until spinach is thawed, about 3 minutes. Stir in the cream and season with nutmeg, salt, and pepper. Spoon the spinach mixture over the tortellini and toss until combined. Top with slices of mozzarella and sprinkle with the pecorino. Bake until browned and bubbling around the edges, about 15 minutes.

VARIATION

Ham, Spinach, and Tortellini Gratin
Sauté 1 cup diced ham with the spinach. Bake as directed above.

Southwest Gratin

This gratin is very spicy and full of great Tex-Mex flavors. For a milder version, substitute plain canned diced tomatoes.

PREP TIME: 10 MINUTES • COOK TIME: 30 MINUTES • MAKES: 4 SERVINGS

Salt
½ pound rigatoni
2 tablespoons extra-virgin olive oil
1 medium zucchini, diced
1 medium yellow onion, chopped
½ pound ground dark-meat turkey
    or ground beef
1 tablespoon minced garlic
1 can (14.5 ounces) diced roasted
    tomatoes with green chiles
¾ cup heavy cream
Freshly ground black pepper
1½ cups crumbled queso fresco
    or feta cheese
1 cup shredded smoked
    mozzarella cheese

1. Heat the oven to 500°F. In a large saucepot over high heat, bring 2 quarts of water to boiling. Add salt to taste and the rigatoni. Cook until almost al dente, about 6 to 8 minutes. Drain well and transfer to a 1½-quart baking dish.

2. Meanwhile, in a large skillet over medium-high heat, heat the olive oil. Add the zucchini, onion, and meat and cook, stirring frequently, until the meat is no longer pink and the onions are soft, 5 to 6 minutes. Stir in the garlic and cook 1 minute longer. Stir in the tomatoes and cream and season with salt and pepper. Bring to a simmer. Toss with the pasta. Sprinkle with the cheeses and bake until browned and bubbling around the edges, about 15 minutes.

Leek and Pasta Bake

Make sure to clean the leeks very well for this casserole. Put the slices in a bowl of cold water and swish them around until they're clean.

PREP TIME: 5 MINUTES • COOK TIME: 35 MINUTES • MAKES: 4 SERVINGS

Salt

12 ounces rigatoni

½ cup mascarpone cheese

2 tablespoons unsalted butter

2 leeks, thinly sliced (white and light green parts) rinsed and drained

Freshly ground black pepper

2 large eggs

1 can (12 ounces) evaporated milk

Pinch cayenne pepper

2 teaspoons lemon juice

2 cups shredded Asiago or Parmesan cheese

1 cup grated pecorino Romano cheese

1. Heat the oven to 350°F. In a large saucepot over high heat, bring 3 quarts of water to boiling. Add salt and the rigatoni. Cook until just al dente, 7 to 9 minutes. Drain well and return to the saucepot. Add the mascarpone and stir until melted.

2. Meanwhile, in a large skillet over medium-high heat, melt the butter. Add the leeks and cook, stirring frequently, until soft, 3 to 4 minutes. Season with salt and pepper and set aside.

3. In a large bowl, mix together the eggs, milk, cayenne, lemon juice, and both cheeses. Season with salt and pepper, stir in the leeks, and pour the mixture over the pasta. Transfer to a 1½-quart ovenproof dish. Bake 5 minutes, stir, and return to the oven. Continue stirring every 5 minutes until the cheese is melted and the mixture is thick, about 20 minutes total.

Pastitsio

Make a Greek salad with cucumbers, tomatoes, and olives to serve alongside this Greek favorite.

PREP TIME: 10 MINUTES • COOK TIME: 30 MINUTES • MAKES: 4 TO 6 SERVINGS

1 medium yellow onion, chopped
Pinch red pepper flakes
1 pound ground beef or lamb
Salt and freshly ground black pepper
1/2 cup sweet Marsala or sherry
Pinch ground cinnamon
1 jar (18 ounces) pasta sauce
12 ounces rigatoni
3 tablespoons unsalted butter
3 tablespoons all-purpose flour
2 cups milk
1 1/4 cups crumbled feta cheese
2 large eggs, beaten
1/2 cup grated Parmesan cheese

1. In a large skillet over medium-high heat, cook the onion, pepper flakes, and meat until browned, 6 to 7 minutes, using a wooden spoon to break up meat. Season with salt and pepper, stir in the Marsala, and simmer 3 to 4 minutes. Stir in the cinnamon and pasta sauce, season with salt and pepper, and simmer 2 to 3 minutes longer. Set aside.

2. Meanwhile, in a large saucepot over high heat, bring 3 quarts water to boiling. Add salt to taste and the rigatoni. Cook until al dente, 7 to 9 minutes. Drain well.

3. Heat the oven to 450°. In a medium saucepan over medium-high heat, melt the butter. Whisk in the flour; simmer 1 minute. Gradually whisk in the milk; simmer 3 minutes. Whisk in the feta until smooth, about 1 minute. Gradually whisk 1 cup of the feta mixture into the eggs, then pour the egg mixture back into the skillet, whisking to mix. Season with salt and pepper and set aside.

4. Pour the meat mixture into a 13 x 9-inch baking dish. Add the pasta and mix lightly. Pour the egg mixture over and sprinkle with the Parmesan. Bake uncovered until bubbling around the edges, 10 to 15 minutes. Let stand 5 minutes before serving.

Baked Rigatoni with Pork

Here's another great dish for entertaining. You can assemble the dish ahead, refrigerate, and bake just before serving. Just remember that it will take a few extra minutes in the oven.

PREP TIME: 10 MINUTES • COOK TIME: 25 MINUTES • MAKES: 6 SERVINGS

Salt
12 ounces rigatoni
2 tablespoons extra-virgin olive oil
1 pound ground pork
Freshly ground black pepper
1 tablespoon minced garlic
½ cup chicken broth
1 cup heavy cream
Pinch saffron
1 teaspoon ground cinnamon
¼ cup chopped Italian parsley
½ teaspoon dried mint
1½ cups shreddedAsiago cheese

1. In a large saucepot over high heat, bring 3 quarts water to boiling. Add salt to taste and the rigatoni. Cook until just al dente, 6 to 8 minutes. Drain and transfer to a 1½-quart baking dish.

2. Meanwhile, in a large skillet over medium-high heat, heat the oil. Add the pork and cook, stirring, until no longer pink, 3 to 4 minutes. Season with salt and pepper and add the garlic. Cook 1 minute longer and stir in the broth, cream, saffron, cinnamon, parsley, and mint. Simmer 3 to 4 minutes and stir in ½ cup Asiago.

3. Heat the oven to 500°F. Pour the cream mixture over the pasta, toss to combine, and top with the remaining Asiago. Bake until browned and bubbling, 10 to 15 minutes.

Pesto Pasta Bake

A green salad or steamed green beans would be a perfect complement to this quick baked pasta.

PREP TIME: 5 MINUTES • COOK TIME: 25 MINUTES • MAKES: 4 SERVINGS

12 ounces rigatoni
Salt
½ cup prepared pesto
¾ cup heavy cream
Freshly ground black pepper
1 ball (about 4 ounces) fresh mozzarella
    cheese, diced
1 cup grated Parmesan cheese

1. Heat the oven to 500°F. In a large saucepot over high heat, bring 3 quarts of water to boiling. Add salt to taste and the rigatoni. Cook until just al dente, 6 to 8 minutes. Drain and transfer to an 8-inch-square baking dish.

2. Meanwhile, in a small bowl, stir together the pesto, cream, salt, and pepper. Pour the pesto mixture over pasta and toss to combine. Top with the mozzarella and sprinkle with the Parmesan. Bake until browned and bubbling, 10 to 15 minutes.

Rigatoni with Tomatoes and Ham

Pick a good-quality smoked ham (I love Applegate Farms Black Forest and Niman Ranch hams) for this very cheesy mac and cheese.

PREP TIME: 5 MINUTES • COOK TIME: 33 MINUTES • MAKES: 4 SERVINGS

Salt
12 ounces rigatoni
½ cup (4 ounces) cream cheese
1 can (12 ounces) evaporated milk
2 large eggs
Pinch cayenne pepper
1 cup canned diced tomatoes, drained
1 cup diced Black Forest ham
Freshly ground black pepper
1 cup grated pecorino Romano cheese
2 cups shredded Cheddar cheese

1. Heat the oven to 350°F. In a large saucepot over high heat, bring 2 quarts of water to boiling. Add salt to taste and the rigatoni. Cook until the rigatoni is still al dente, 6 to 8 minutes. Drain well and return to the saucepot. Add the cream cheese and stir until melted.

2. Meanwhile, mix the milk, eggs, cayenne, tomatoes, ham, salt, pepper, and the cheeses in a large bowl. Pour over the pasta, toss, and transfer to a 1½-quart heatproof dish. Bake 5 minutes, stir, and bake another 5 minutes. Stir again and bake 10 to 15 minutes longer or until thickened and creamy.

Baked Spaghetti Ring

This is a simple dish, but it looks very impressive.

PREP TIME: 5 MINUTES • COOK TIME: 25 MINUTES • MAKES: 6 SERVINGS

Salt
12 ounces spaghetti
3 tablespoons unsalted butter
1 large egg, lightly beaten
¼ cup grated Parmesan cheese, plus more
    for garnish
Freshly ground black pepper
3 tablespoons extra-virgin olive oil
1 ball (about 4 ounces) fresh mozzarella
    cheese, thinly sliced
1 tablespoon minced garlic
½ teaspoon fennel seeds
Pinch red pepper flakes
1 can (15 ounces) tomato sauce
1 can (15 ounces) diced Italian tomatoes
Basil sprigs, for garnish

1. In a large saucepot over high heat, bring 2 quarts of water to boiling. Add salt to taste and the spaghetti and cook until almost al dente, 6 to 8 minutes. Drain and transfer to a large bowl. Stir in the butter, egg, and ¼ cup Parmesan. Season with salt and pepper.

2. Heat the oven to 500°F. Grease a 6-cup ring mold with 1 tablespoon olive oil and pack half the spaghetti into it. Cover with the mozzarella and top with the remaining spaghetti. Bake until browned and bubbling, about 15 minutes.

3. Meanwhile, in a large skillet over medium-high heat, heat the remaining 2 tablespoons oil. Add the garlic, fennel, and pepper flakes and cook 30 seconds. Stir in the tomato sauce and tomatoes. Season with salt and pepper and simmer 2 to 3 minutes.

4. To serve, run a dull knife between the sides of mold and the spaghetti to loosen. Cover mold with a warm platter, invert, and carefully lift mold off pasta. Pour the tomato sauce into the middle. Sprinkle with additional Parmesan and garnish with the basil sprigs.

Parmesan Mac & Cheese

Buy the best-quality shredded Parmesan for the best flavor.

PREP TIME: 5 MINUTES • COOK TIME: 30 MINUTES • MAKES: 4 TO 6 SERVINGS

½ pound elbow macaroni
Salt
½ cup mascarpone cheese
2 large eggs
1 can (12 ounces) evaporated milk
Pinch cayenne pepper
2 teaspoons lemon juice
2 cups shredded Parmesan cheese
1 cup grated pecorino Romano cheese

1. Heat the oven to 350°F. In a large saucepot over high heat, bring 2 quarts water to boiling. Add salt to taste and the macaroni. Cook until the macaroni is still al dente, 6 to 8 minutes. Drain well and return to the saucepot. Add the mascarpone and stir until melted.

2. Meanwhile, in a large bowl, mix together the eggs, milk, cayenne, lemon juice, and cheeses. Pour mixture over the pasta, toss, and transfer to a 1½-quart ovenproof dish. Bake 5 minutes, stir, and return to the oven. Continue stirring every 5 minutes until the cheese is melted and the mixture is thick, about 20 minutes total.

VARIATION

Mac & Cheese with Garlic Crumbs
Prepare recipe as directed above. While macaroni is baking, in a medium skillet over medium-high heat, melt 2 tablespoons unsalted butter. Add 1 tablespoon minced garlic and cook 1 minute. Stir in 1 cup fresh bread crumbs and a large pinch of salt. Cook, stirring frequently, until toasted, 2 to 3 minutes. Sprinkle over the macaroni when it is finished baking and serve.

Baked Pasta with Butternut Squash

Peeling and chopping butternut squash is quite time-consuming. Frozen butternut squash cubes are a good substitute for fresh and work perfectly in this rosemary-scented bake.

PREP TIME: 5 MINUTES • COOK TIME: 25 MINUTES • MAKES: 4 SERVINGS

Salt
1 pound farfalle
2 tablespoons extra-virgin olive oil
2 tablespoons unsalted butter
1 package (10 ounces) frozen butternut
squash cubes
1 tablespoon minced garlic
½ teaspoon dried rosemary
Pinch red pepper flakes
Freshly ground black pepper
1 cup chicken broth
1 cup heavy cream
1 cup shredded Asiago
cheese

1. Heat the oven to 500°F. In a large saucepot over high heat, bring 4 quarts of water to boiling. Add salt to taste and the farfalle. Cook until just al dente, 6 to 8 minutes. Drain and transfer to a 1½-quart baking dish.

2. Meanwhile, in a large skillet over medium-high heat, heat the oil and butter. Add the squash, garlic, rosemary, pepper flakes, salt, pepper, broth, and cream. Simmer until lightly thickened, about 2 minutes. Pour the sauce over the farfalle and toss to coat. Sprinkle with the cheese. Bake until browned and bubbling around the edges, 10 to 15 minutes.

Baked Shells with Mushroom Sauce

There's no need to stuff the shells in this casserole; the filling and sauce are combined and just poured over the top.

PREP TIME: 5 MINUTES • COOK TIME: 25 MINUTES • MAKES: 8 SERVINGS

Salt
12 ounces large pasta shells
4 tablespoons unsalted butter
2 packages sliced cremini mushrooms
1 tablespoon minced garlic
¼ teaspoon dried thyme
Freshly ground black pepper
1 cup heavy cream
12 ounces crumbled fresh goat cheese
1 can (28 ounces) diced Italian tomatoes
1 cup shredded pecorino Romano cheese

1. Heat the oven to 500°F. In a large saucepot over high heat, bring 3 quarts of water to boiling. Add salt to taste and the shells. Cook until almost al dente, 7 to 9 minutes. Drain well and transfer to a 13 x 9-inch baking dish.

2. Meanwhile, in a large skillet over high heat, heat the butter. Add the mushrooms and cook until browned and tender, about 5 minutes. Add the garlic and thyme and cook 1 minute longer. Season with salt and pepper. Stir in the cream, half the goat cheese, and the tomatoes. Bring to a simmer.

3. Pour the mushroom sauce over the pasta. Sprinkle with the remaining goat cheese and the pecorino. Bake until bubbling around the edges, about 10 minutes.

Baked Shells with Herbed Ricotta

Any variety of spiced and herbed cheese will work well in this casserole.

PREP TIME: 15 MINUTES • COOK TIME: 30 MINUTES • MAKES: 6 SERVINGS

Salt

12 ounces large pasta shells

2 tablespoons extra-virgin olive oil

1 tablespoon minced garlic

Pinch red pepper flakes

$\frac{1}{3}$ cup white wine

1 jar (25 ounces) pasta sauce

15 ounces ricotta cheese

8 ounces herb cheese

3 tablespoons chopped Italian parsley

1 large egg

Freshly ground black pepper

1$\frac{1}{2}$ cups shredded pecorino Romano cheese

1. Heat the oven to 450°F. In a large saucepot over high heat, bring 2 quarts of water to boiling. Add salt to taste and the shells. Cook until almost al dente, 7 to 9 minutes. Drain, rinse with cold water, and set aside.

2. Meanwhile, in a large skillet over high heat, heat the oil. Add the garlic and pepper flakes and cook 30 seconds. Add the wine and simmer 1 minute. Stir in the pasta sauce. Bring to simmering and season with salt and pepper. Remove from heat.

3. In a small bowl, mix together the ricotta, herb cheese, parsley, and egg. Season with salt and pepper.

4. Place the cooked shells on the bottom of a 13 x 9-inch baking dish. Spoon the cheese mixture over the shells and sprinkle with $\frac{1}{2}$ cup of the pecorino. Pour the tomato mixture over, sprinkle with the remaining pecorino, and cover with foil. Bake until sauce is bubbling, about 20 minutes.

Baked Scampi Ziti

To make sure the shrimp don't get overcooked, barely simmer them before the dish is assembled and baked.

PREP TIME: 10 MINUTES • **COOK TIME: 30 MINUTES** • **MAKES: 4 TO 6 SERVINGS**

Salt
1 pound ziti
¼ cup extra-virgin olive oil
4 tablespoons unsalted butter
2 tablespoons minced garlic
Pinch red pepper flakes
½ cup white wine
3 cups canned diced Italian tomatoes
1 pound medium peeled shrimp
½ cup chopped Italian parsley
Freshly ground black pepper
1½ cups crumbled goat cheese or feta or
   a combination of both

1. Heat the oven to 450°F. In a large saucepot over high heat, bring 4 quarts of water to boiling. Add salt to taste and the ziti. Cook until almost al dente, 6 to 8 minutes. Drain well.

2. Meanwhile, in a large skillet over high heat, heat the oil and the butter. Add the garlic and pepper flakes and cook 30 seconds. Stir in the wine and simmer 1 minute. Add the tomatoes, shrimp, and parsley and simmer 2 minutes longer. Season with salt and pepper and pour into a 1½-quart baking dish. Add the ziti and toss. Crumble the cheese over, cover dish with foil, and bake until bubbling around the edges, 15 to 20 minutes.

Baked Ziti with Roasted Pepper Cream

You may use any type of short pasta in this easy and very rich baked dish.

PREP TIME: 15 MINUTES • COOK TIME: 30 MINUTES • MAKES: 6 SERVINGS

Salt
1 pound ziti
1 jar (16 ounces) roasted red peppers,
   drained
1 jar (25 ounces) tomato pasta sauce
1 cup heavy cream
Freshly ground black pepper
1 cup shredded mozzarella cheese
1 cup grated Parmesan cheese

1. Heat the oven to 425°F. In a large saucepot over high heat, bring 4 quarts of water to boiling. Add salt to taste and the ziti. Cook until almost al dente, 6 to 8 minutes. Drain and return the ziti to the saucepot.

2. Meanwhile, purée the peppers in a food processor fitted with a metal blade until smooth. Add the tomato sauce and cream and purée until mixed. Season with salt and pepper. Pour mixture over the ziti and toss to combine. Transfer to a 3-quart baking dish. Sprinkle with both the cheeses and bake until bubbling around the edges, 20 to 25 minutes.

Tex-Mex Baked Ravioli

This mildly spiced bake is fine for kids and adults alike, but if you'd prefer more heat, use spicy instead of medium salsa.

PREP TIME: 10 MINUTES • COOK TIME: 30 MINUTES • MAKES: 6 SERVINGS

3 tablespoons unsalted butter
1 large red onion, chopped
½ teaspoon ground cumin
2 cups ricotta cheese
1½ cups crumbled queso fresco or feta
    cheese
Salt and freshly ground black pepper
½ cup heavy cream
1 can (15 ounces) tomato sauce
1 jar (15 ounces) medium chipotle salsa
Olive oil spray
2 packages (8 to 10 ounces each) fresh
    cheese ravioli
2 cups shredded mozzarella
    cheese

1. Heat the oven to 500°F. In a large skillet over medium-high heat, melt the butter. Add the onion and cook until lightly browned, 5 to 6 minutes. Stir in the cumin and cook 1 minute longer. Spoon mixture into a medium bowl. Stir in the ricotta and 1 cup of the queso fresco. Season with salt and pepper. In a separate bowl, stir together the cream, tomato sauce, and salsa.

2. Spray a 13 x 9-inch baking dish with the olive oil spray. Spread ¼ cup of the tomato sauce on the bottom. Cover with half the ravioli and all the ricotta. Top ricotta with the remaining ravioli. Pour the remaining tomato sauce over the ravioli. Sprinkle with the remaining queso fresco and the mozzarella. Bake until browned and bubbling around the edges, 15 to 20 minutes.

Ravioli with Cauliflower and Caper Sauce

Serve this elegant dish with a lightly dressed green salad, an assortment of antipasti, and bread. It's a great dinner, and perfect for entertaining.

PREP TIME: 5 MINUTES   •   COOK TIME: 10 MINUTES   •   MAKES: 4 SERVINGS

Salt
2 packages (9 to 10 ounces each) fresh
   cheese ravioli
6 tablespoons unsalted butter
2 tablespoons extra-virgin olive oil
1 tablespoon minced garlic
Pinch red pepper flakes
1 package (10 ounces) frozen chopped
   cauliflower
2 tablespoons capers, drained
Freshly ground black pepper
Basil leaves, roughly chopped, for garnish
Grated Asiago cheese, for serving

1. In a large saucepot over high heat, bring 4 quarts of water to boiling. Add salt to taste and the ravioli. Cook until tender, 3 to 5 minutes. Drain well and transfer to a large serving bowl.

2. In a large skillet over medium-high heat, melt the butter and oil. Add the garlic and pepper flakes and cook 1 minute. Stir in the cauliflower and cook until cauliflower is tender and garlic is lightly golden, 7 to 8 minutes. Stir in the capers. Season with salt and pepper. Pour sauce over the ravioli and toss to coat. Sprinkle with the chopped basil leaves and serve with Asiago on the side.

VARIATION

Ravioli with Cauliflower, Caper, and Tomato Sauce
Add 3 seeded and diced plum tomatoes to the cauliflower along with the capers. Cook 1 minute longer.

Spinach Ravioli with Sausage and Red Peppers

Lightly spiked with orange, this sauce is great on fettuccine as well. Use a vegetable peeler to cut wide strips of orange zest.

PREP TIME: 5 MINUTES • COOK TIME: 15 MINUTES • MAKES: 4 SERVINGS

Salt
2 packages (9 ounces each) fresh spinach
   ravioli
2 tablespoons extra-virgin olive oil
½ pound mild bulk Italian sausage
1 tablespoon minced garlic
1 can (15 ounces) diced Italian tomatoes
1 jar (12 ounces) roasted peppers, drained
   and chopped
2 strips (2 x 1-inch) orange zest
½ cup heavy cream
Freshly ground black pepper
Shredded Asiago or Parmesan cheese,
   for serving

1. In a large saucepot over high heat, bring 4 quarts water to boiling. Add salt to taste and the ravioli. Cook until tender, 3 to 5 minutes. Drain and transfer to serving dishes.

2. Meanwhile, in a large skillet over medium-high heat, heat the oil. Add the sausage and cook, breaking up any clumps, until no longer pink, 4 to 5 minutes. Add the garlic and cook 1 minute. Stir in the tomatoes, peppers, orange zest, and cream. Season with salt and pepper. Simmer until lightly thickened, 3 to 4 minutes, scraping up any browned bits that cling to the pan. To serve, remove the orange zest strips. Spoon the sauce over the ravioli and serve with shredded cheese on the side.

Cheese Ravioli with Ham and Asparagus

Buy medium-thick (not thin) asparagus with tightly closed tops for this dish. Shop for asparagus stored with the stems in water for the freshest flavor.

PREP TIME: 5 MINUTES • COOK TIME: 10 MINUTES • MAKES: 4 SERVINGS

Salt
2 packages (9 to 10 ounces each) fresh
   cheese ravioli
1 pound asparagus, woody ends trimmed
3 tablespoons unsalted butter
1 cup heavy cream
1 cup diced ham
½ cup chicken broth
1 tablespoon chopped fresh tarragon
Freshly ground black pepper
½ cup grated Parmesan cheese, plus more
   for serving

1. In a large saucepot over high heat, bring 4 quarts of water to boiling. Add salt to taste and the ravioli. Cook until tender, 3 to 5 minutes. Drain and transfer to serving dishes.

2. Meanwhile, cut the asparagus diagonally into 1-inch pieces; set aside. In a large skillet over medium-high heat, melt the butter. Add the asparagus, cream, ham, broth, and tarragon and bring to boiling. Reduce heat and simmer until asparagus is tender and sauce is slightly thickened, 5 to 6 minutes. Season with salt and pepper and stir in ½ cup Parmesan cheese. To serve, spoon the asparagus sauce over the pasta and sprinkle with additional cheese.

Ravioli with Sage, Pancetta, and Peas

Orechiette or tortellini are both good substitutes for the ravioli in this dish.

PREP TIME: 5 MINUTES • COOK TIME: 12 MINUTES • MAKES: 4 SERVINGS

Salt
2 packages (9 to 10 ounces each) fresh
   cheese ravioli
2 tablespoons unsalted butter
4 ounces pancetta or 4 thick slices bacon,
   chopped
12 fresh sage leaves
2 cups frozen baby peas
Pinch red pepper flakes
¼ cup heavy cream
Freshly ground black pepper
Grated Parmesan cheese, for serving

1. In a large saucepot over high heat, bring 4 quarts water to boiling. Add salt to taste and the ravioli. Cook until tender, 3 to 5 minutes. Drain and transfer to a large serving bowl.

2. Meanwhile, in a large skillet over medium-high heat, melt the butter. Add the pancetta or bacon and cook until crisp, about 8 minutes. Using a slotted spoon, transfer to a paper towel-lined plate. Add the sage to the pan and cook until it is crisp and turns grey, about 30 seconds to 1 minute. Using a slotted spoon, transfer to the same plate.

3. Add the peas, pepper flakes, and cream to the skillet. Cook until peas are tender, 2 to 3 minutes. Season with salt and pepper. Pour the mixture over the pasta, toss, and sprinkle with the sage leaves and pancetta. Serve with Parmesan on the side.

Ravioli with Smoked Salmon Wasabi Butter

As this is quite rich, it makes a great first course. If you have difficulty finding smoked salmon in cans, substitute 1 cup diced lox ends or flaked hot-smoked salmon.

PREP TIME: 10 MINUTES • COOK TIME: 5 MINUTES • MAKES: 6 TO 8 SERVINGS

Salt
3 packages (9 to 10 ounces each) fresh
    cheese ravioli
1 stick unsalted butter, softened
1 tablespoon lemon juice
1 teaspoon grated lemon zest
1 teaspoon wasabi paste
Freshly ground black pepper
1 can (6.5 ounces) smoked Alaskan
    salmon, drained and flaked
1 bunch scallions, thinly sliced
Basil leaves, roughly chopped, for garnish

1. In a large saucepot over high heat, bring 4 quarts of water to boiling. Add salt to taste and the ravioli. Cook until tender, 3 to 5 minutes. Drain.

2. Meanwhile, in the bowl of a food processor with the steel blade attached, combine the butter, lemon juice, zest, wasabi, a pinch of salt, and $\frac{1}{2}$ teaspoon pepper. Process until well mixed. Using a spatula, transfer mixture to a large serving bowl. Stir in the salmon and scallions. Add the ravioli and toss until well coated. Transfer to serving dishes and garnish with basil.

Ravioli with Herbs

This makes a wonderful appetizer, brunch, or light lunch dish.

PREP TIME: 5 MINUTES • COOK TIME: 10 MINUTES • MAKES: 4 SERVINGS

Salt

2 packages (9 to 10 ounces each) fresh
cheese ravioli

2 tablespoons unsalted butter

4 tablespoons garlic-flavored or lemon-
flavored olive oil

1 cup packed basil leaves, torn

½ cup sliced scallions

½ teaspoon dried oregano

Freshly ground black pepper

Grated Parmesan or Asiago cheese, for
serving

1. In a large saucepot over high heat, bring 4 quarts of water to boiling. Add salt to taste and the ravioli. Cook until tender, 3 to 5 minutes. Drain well and transfer to a large serving bowl.

2. Meanwhile, in a large skillet over medium heat, heat the butter, olive oil, basil, scallions, and oregano just until the butter melts. Stir in salt and pepper. Pour the butter mixture over the pasta, toss to coat, and serve with grated cheese on the side.

Ravioli in Garlic and Zucchini Broth

If you have it on hand, use homemade broth in this very simple dish. Otherwise, broth from an aseptic container is the best bet.

PREP TIME: 5 MINUTES • COOK TIME: 20 MINUTES • MAKES: 4 SERVINGS

2 cups chicken broth
4 cloves garlic, peeled but left whole
2 tablespoons unsalted butter
Salt and freshly ground black pepper
2 packages (9 to 10 ounces each) fresh
    cheese ravioli
1 medium zucchini (about 8 ounces), cut
    in half lengthwise and thinly sliced
Grated Parmesan cheese, for serving

1. In a medium saucepan over high heat ring the chicken broth and garlic to boiling. Reduce heat to medium-low and simmer until liquid is reduced to $\frac{1}{2}$ cup, about 20 minutes. Using a wooden spoon, mash the garlic into the broth and whisk in the butter. Season with salt and pepper.

2. Meanwhile, in a large saucepot over high heat, bring 4 quarts of water to boiling. Add salt to taste, the ravioli, and the zucchini. Cook until tender, 3 to 5 minutes. Drain well and transfer to a large serving bowl. Pour the reduced broth over, toss, and serve with Parmesan and additional pepper on the side.

Ravioli in Mushroom Broth

For a slightly lighter broth, substitute vegetable or chicken broth for the beef broth in this dish.

PREP TIME: 10 MINUTES • COOK TIME: 16 MINUTES • MAKES: 4 SERVINGS

½ ounce dried porcini mushrooms, rinsed
Salt
2 packages (8 to 10 ounces each) fresh
   beef, cheese, or mushroom ravioli
2 tablespoons extra-virgin olive oil
1 package (8 ounces) sliced white or
   cremini mushrooms
1 tablespoon minced garlic
Pinch red pepper flakes
1 can (15 ounces) beef broth
¼ teaspoon dried thyme
Freshly ground black pepper
Grated Parmesan cheese, for serving

1. Combine the porcini and 1 cup water in a glass measuring cup. Microwave on high power 1 minute. Let stand 10 minutes. Pour the porcini through a fine sieve, reserving the soaking liquid. Coarsely chop the porcini.

2. Meanwhile, in a large saucepot over high heat, bring 4 quarts of water to boiling. Add salt to taste and the ravioli. Cook until tender, 3 to 5 minutes. Divide the ravioli among four soup plates.

3. In a large saucepan over medium-high heat, heat the oil. Add the sliced mushrooms and porcini and cook until fresh mushrooms are browned and tender, 5 to 6 minutes. Add the garlic and pepper flakes and cook 1 minute longer. Stir in the broth and the thyme. Carefully pour in the mushroom soaking liquid, stopping before pouring any grit into the pot. Bring to a simmer. To serve, ladle the broth and mushrooms over the ravioli. Sprinkle with pepper and Parmesan and serve immediately.

Tortellini with Artichoke Mascarpone Sauce

This easy sauce is also perfect on ravioli.

PREP TIME: 5 MINUTES • COOK TIME: 10 MINUTES • MAKES: 4 SERVINGS

Salt
2 packages (9 to 10 ounces each) fresh
   cheese tortellini
2 tablespoons unsalted butter
1 tablespoon minced garlic
Pinch red pepper flakes
1 jar (12 ounces) marinated artichokes,
   drained and chopped
½ cup mascarpone cheese
¼ cup heavy cream
⅓ cup chicken broth
Freshly ground black pepper
2 tablespoons chopped Italian parsley
Grated Asiago or Parmesan cheese,
   for serving

1. In a large saucepot over high heat, bring 4 quarts water to boiling. Add salt to taste and the tortellini. Cook until tender, 3 to 5 minutes. Drain and transfer to serving dishes.

2. Meanwhile, in a large skillet over medium-high heat, melt the butter. Add the garlic and pepper flakes and cook 30 seconds. Add the artichokes, mascarpone, cream, and broth. Season with salt and pepper. Simmer until lightly thickened, 2 to 3 minutes. Stir in the parsley. Spoon sauce over the pasta, sprinkle with cheese, and serve.

Two-Toned Tortellini with Gorgonzola Sauce

You don't have to use both spinach and plain tortellini in this dish, but the two colors are very festive. Serve a bitter lettuce salad (such as frisée or endive) with this rich dish.

PREP TIME: 5 MINUTES • COOK TIME: 10 MINUTES • MAKES: 4 SERVINGS

Salt

2 packages (9 to 10 ounces each, 1 spinach and 1 plain) fresh cheese tortellini

1 cup (about 3 ounces) crumbled Gorgonzola or blue cheese

½ cup mascarpone cheese

2 tablespoons grated Parmesan cheese, plus more for garnish

1 teaspoon grated lemon zest

Freshly ground black pepper

1. In a large saucepot over high heat, bring 4 quarts water to boiling. Add salt to taste and the tortellini. Cook until tender, 3 to 5 minutes. Reserve 3 tablespoons of cooking water and drain.

2. Meanwhile, in a large serving bowl, mix together the Gorgonzola, mascarpone, 2 tablespoons of the Parmesan, lemon zest, and salt and pepper. Add 2 tablespoons cooking water and the tortellini and toss until mixed, adding more cooking water if the mixture seems dry. Divide among four serving plates. Sprinkle with additional Parmesan and serve.

Tortellini with Greek Yogurt Sauce

Greek yogurt is amazingly creamy and very, very thick. If it's unavailable, substitute full-fat plain yogurt. This tastes best with lots of Parmesan.

PREP TIME: 5 MINUTES • COOK TIME: 10 MINUTES • MAKES: 2 TO 3 SERVINGS

Salt
1 package (9 to 10 ounces) fresh cheese
   tortellini
4 tablespoons unsalted butter
1 cup chopped yellow onion
1 tablespoon minced garlic
½ cup Greek or full-fat plain yogurt
Freshly ground black pepper
Grated Parmesan cheese, for serving

1. In a large saucepot over high heat, bring 2 quarts of water to boiling. Add salt to taste and the tortellini. Cook until tender, 3 to 5 minutes. Drain and transfer to a serving bowl.

2. Meanwhile, in a medium skillet over high heat, melt the butter. Add the onion and cook until lightly browned, 4 to 5 minutes. Stir in the garlic and cook 1 minute longer. Spoon mixture over tortellini, add the yogurt, salt, and pepper, and toss until coated. Serve with Parmesan on the side.

Everyday Pasta

Fennel, Red Pepper, and Sausage Rigatoni

If you can find a jar of roasted red and yellow peppers with garlic, use it here—it will make this already tasty dish even prettier and more flavorful.

PREP TIME: 5 MINUTES • **COOK TIME: 20 MINUTES** • **MAKES: 4 SERVINGS**

Salt
1 pound rigatoni
2 tablespoons extra-virgin olive oil
1 pound spicy bulk pork sausage
1 fennel bulb, coarsely chopped
    (about 1¼ cups)
1 jar (12 ounces) roasted red peppers
    with garlic, drained and chopped
¼ cup chopped Italian parsley
Freshly ground black pepper
½ cup grated Asiago cheese, plus more
    for garnish

1. In a large saucepot over high heat, bring 4 quarts of water to boiling. Add salt to taste and the rigatoni. Cook until al dente, 7 to 9 minutes, and drain.

2. Meanwhile, in a large skillet over medium-high heat, heat the oil. Add the sausage and cook, stirring frequently, until browned and cooked through, 4 to 5 minutes. Stir in the fennel, 1 cup water, and peppers. Cook until the fennel is soft, about 5 minutes. Season with salt and set aside.

3. Transfer the rigatoni to a bowl and pour the fennel mixture over. Add the parsley, black pepper, and ½ cup Asiago, and toss until mixed. Season with salt and pepper and serve with additional Asiago on the side.

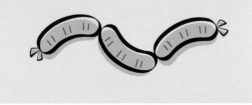

Bucatini with Fennel, Onions, and Olives

Use your food processor's slicing blade to slice the fennel and onions.

PREP TIME: 10 MINUTES • COOK TIME: 25 MINUTES • MAKES: 4 SERVINGS

Salt
1 pound bucatini
¼ cup extra-virgin olive oil
1 fennel bulb, tops cut off and reserved,
    bulb thinly sliced
1 large onion, thinly sliced
Pinch fennel seeds
Pinch red pepper flakes
¼ cup pitted Kalamata olives, chopped
1 tablespoon capers, drained
1 cup chicken broth
1 cup shredded Parmesan cheese
Freshly ground black pepper

1. In a large saucepot over high heat, bring 4 quarts of water to boiling. Add salt to taste and the bucatini. Cook until al dente, 7 to 9 minutes. Drain the bucatini and return it to the saucepot.

2. In a large skillet over medium heat, heat the oil. Add the sliced fennel, onion, fennel seeds, and pepper flakes. Season with salt and cook, stirring frequently, until the fennel and onion are very soft but not browned, about 10 minutes. Stir in the olives, capers, and broth and bring to a simmer. Cook, stirring occasionally, until broth has slightly reduced, 7 to 8 minutes. Chop 2 tablespoons of the reserved fennel fronds and stir in.

3. Pour the fennel mixture over the bucatini, add half the Parmesan, and toss until mixed. Divide among serving dishes. Serve warm with the remaining Parmesan and black pepper on the side.

Radiatore with Herbed Ricotta

Shredding basil is super easy: just stack several leaves and roll them into a cigar shape, then cut crosswise into strips.

PREP TIME: 5 MINUTES • COOK TIME: 10 MINUTES • MAKES: 4 SERVINGS

1 pound radiatore

Salt

1 container (15 ounces) whole milk
    ricotta cheese

¼ cup grated Parmesan cheese

¼ cup grated pecorino Romano cheese

Freshly ground black pepper

2 tablespoons heavy cream

1 cup shredded basil

1. In a large saucepot over high heat, bring 4 quarts of water to boiling. Add salt to taste and the radiatore. Cook until the radiatore is al dente, 7 to 9 minutes. Reserve ¼ cup cooking water and drain well.

2. Meanwhile, in a large bowl, stir together the remaining ingredients. Add the hot pasta and toss until mixed, adding cooking water if the mixture seems dry. Season with salt and pepper and serve.

VARIATION

**Radiatore with Herbed Ricotta
and Sun-Dried Tomatoes**
Stir in ¼ cup chopped sun-dried tomatoes in oil along with the pasta.

Gemelli with Chicken and Feta Cheese

If I don't have leftover chicken, I buy a roasted one from my supermarket's deli. Two breasts or 4 thighs should give you the 2 cups of diced chicken that you need.

PREP TIME: 10 MINUTES • **COOK TIME: 10 MINUTES** • **MAKES: 4 SERVINGS**

Salt
1 pound gemelli
1 jar (10.5 ounces) marinated feta cheese
1 teaspoon minced garlic
½ cup thinly sliced scallions (about 5)
2 cups diced cooked chicken
2 tablespoons capers
1 cup coarsely chopped basil
1 tablespoon balsamic vinegar
Freshly ground black pepper

1. In a large saucepot over high heat, bring 4 quarts of water to boiling. Add salt to taste and the gemell. Cook until al dente, 7 to 9 minutes. Drain well.

2. Drain 2 tablespoons of the oil from the marinated feta and pour into a large bowl. Discard the remaining oil. Add the feta, garlic, scallions, chicken, capers, basil, and vinegar to the oil and toss to combine. Add the gemelli and toss until combined. Season with salt and pepper and divide among serving dishes. Serve warm.

Creamy Garlic Pasta with Sugar Snaps

Celentani are loose corkscrew pasta. Good substitutes are fusilli or rotini.

PREP TIME: 5 MINUTES • COOK TIME: 15 MINUTES • MAKES: 4 SERVINGS

Salt
8 ounces celentani
¼ cup garlic-flavored olive oil
1 tablespoon minced garlic
½ cup thinly sliced scallions (about 5)
1 bag (8 ounces) washed and trimmed
    sugar snap peas
½ cup white wine or chicken broth
1 teaspoon dried mint
2 cups (packed) washed spinach
1½ cups (6 ounces) feta cheese crumbles
Freshly ground black pepper

1. In a large saucepot over high heat, bring 2 quarts of water to boiling. Add salt to taste and the celentani. Cook until al dente, 6 to 8 minutes. Reserve ½ cup of the cooking water and drain.

2. In a large skillet over medium-high heat, heat the oil. Add the garlic and scallions and cook 30 seconds. Stir in the sugar snaps and wine or broth and simmer, stirring frequently, until almost tender, about 4 minutes. Stir in the mint and spinach and toss.

3. Add the celentani to the skillet and stir in 1 cup of the feta cheese. Simmer, stirring, until the feta melts and a creamy sauce forms, adding more cooking water if necessary. Season with salt and pepper and divide among serving dishes. Sprinkle with the remaining ½ cup feta and serve.

Wagon Wheels with Kielbasa and Chickpeas

Kids love both the flavors and shapes of this fast pasta.

PREP TIME: 5 MINUTES • COOK TIME: 10 MINUTES • MAKES: 6 SERVINGS

Salt
1 pound wagon wheel pasta
¼ cup extra-virgin olive oil
1 pound kielbasa, sliced into ½-inch rounds
1 tablespoon minced garlic
Pinch red pepper flakes
1 bunch (about 8) scallions, thinly sliced
1 can (15 ounces) chickpeas, drained and
    rinsed
4 cups (packed) washed spinach
Freshly ground black pepper
Grated pecorino Romano cheese, for
    serving

1. In a large saucepot over high heat, bring 4 quarts of water to boiling. Add salt to taste and the pasta. Cook until al dente, 7 to 8 minutes. Reserve ½ cup cooking water, drain the pasta, and return it to the saucepot.

2. In a large skillet over medium-high heat, heat 1 tablespoon of the oil. Add the kielbasa and cook until browned, about 5 minutes, stirring frequently.

3. Add the remaining olive oil, the garlic, pepper flakes, and scallions and cook 1 minute. Stir in the chickpeas and the spinach and stir until mixed.

4. Pour the sausage mixture over the pasta. Add half the cooking water and cook over medium-high heat, stirring constantly until the ingredients are well combined and a sauce has formed, adding more water if necessary. Season with salt and pepper. Serve with grated pecorino on the side.

Four-Cheese Pasta with Smoked Chicken

Just about any four-cheese shredded blend will be fabulous in this creamy pasta.

PREP TIME: 5 MINUTES • COOK TIME: 20 MINUTES • MAKES: 4 TO 6 SERVINGS

Salt
12 ounces cavatelli or radiatore
3 tablespoons unsalted butter
3 large eggs
1 can (12 ounces) evaporated milk
Pinch cayenne
½ teaspoon Dijon mustard
1½ cups diced smoked chicken
12 ounces shredded four-cheese mix
   (Parmesan, Asiago, fontina, and
   provolone)
Freshly ground black pepper

1. In a large saucepot over high heat, bring 3 quarts of water to boiling. Add salt to taste and the pasta. Cook until the pasta is just al dente, 7 to 9 minutes. Drain well and return it to the saucepot. Reduce heat to medium-low. Add the butter and stir until melted.

2. Meanwhile, in a large bowl, mix together the eggs, milk, cayenne, mustard, chicken, and grated cheeses. Pour over the pasta and stir until the cheese is melted and the mixture begins to thicken, 7 to 10 minutes. (Don't let the mixture boil or it will get grainy.) Season with salt and pepper and serve.

VARIATION

Four-Cheese Pasta with Smoked Chicken and Broccoli
Cook the pasta until still a little crunchy, about 5 minutes. Add 2 cups frozen chopped broccoli and cook 2 minutes longer. Continue as directed above.

Pasta with Prosciutto and Green Beans

You can substitute Black Forest ham for the prosciutto here.

PREP TIME: 5 MINUTES • COOK TIME: 10 MINUTES • MAKES: 4 SERVINGS

Salt
12 ounces radiatore or fusilli
¼ cup extra-virgin olive oil
2 cups frozen cut green beans
Pinch red pepper flakes
½ cup thinly sliced prosciutto (about
    2 ounces)
Freshly ground black pepper
1 cup grated Parmesan cheese

1. In a large saucepot over high heat, bring 2 quarts of water to boiling. Add salt to taste and the pasta. Cook until al dente, 7 to 9 minutes. Reserve ½ cup cooking water and drain well.

2. In a large skillet over medium-high heat, heat the oil. Add the green beans, pepper flakes, and salt. Cook, stirring frequently, until beans are tender, 5 to 6 minutes. Stir in the prosciutto and cook 1 minute longer.

3. Add the pasta and half the cooking water to the skillet. Add ½ cup Parmesan and toss until combined. Cook 1 minute longer, adding more cooking water if the mixture seems dry. Season with black pepper and serve with the remaining Parmesan on the side.

Watercress, Bacon, and Shrimp Pasta

You can substitute ¼ cup of orange juice for the orange oil and eliminate the water from the recipe. Add the juice to the skillet before the shrimp and simmer it 2 minutes to reduce it slightly.

PREP TIME: 5 MINUTES • COOK TIME: 20 MINUTES • MAKES: 2 GENEROUS SERVINGS

Salt
8 ounces orecchiette
4 slices bacon
2 tablespoons orange-flavored olive oil
Pinch red pepper flakes
Grated zest of 1 orange
1 tablespoon minced garlic
¾ pound small shelled and deveined frozen shrimp, thawed
1 bunch watercress, tough stems removed, coarsely chopped
Freshly ground black pepper

1. In a large saucepot over high heat, bring 2 quarts of water to boiling. Add salt to taste and the orecchiette. Cook until al dente, 7 to 9 minutes. Drain and transfer to a large serving bowl.

2. Meanwhile, in a large skillet over medium-high heat, cook the bacon until crisp, about 8 minutes. Remove to a paper towel-lined plate. Discard all but 2 tablespoons of the bacon fat from the pan. Chop or crumble the bacon into small pieces.

3. In the same skillet, combine the orange oil, 2 tablespoons of water, the pepper flakes, orange zest, garlic, and shrimp and cook until just opaque, about 2 minutes. Add the shrimp mixture, the watercress, and the crumbled bacon to the orecchiette. Season with salt and pepper, toss until combined, and serve immediately.

Pasta with Kale, White Beans, and Anchovies

The easiest way to wash kale is to shred it first, then throw the shreds into a sink or salad spinner filled with cold water.

PREP TIME: 15 MINUTES • COOK TIME: 15 MINUTES • MAKES: 4 TO 6 SERVINGS

Salt

1 pound campanelle or orecchiette

½ pound kale, tough ribs removed, shredded

⅓ cup extra-virgin olive oil

1 tablespoon minced garlic

Pinch red pepper flakes

4 anchovy fillets, chopped

1 can (15 ounces) white beans, drained and rinsed

Freshly ground black pepper

Grated pecorino Romano cheese, for serving

1. In a large saucepot over high heat, bring 4 quarts of water to boiling. Add salt to taste and the pasta. Cook 4 minutes and add the kale. Continue cooking until the pasta is a very crunchy al dente, 5 to 7 minutes. Reserve 1 cup of the cooking water. Drain the pasta and kale and return them to the saucepot.

2. Meanwhile, in a large skillet over medium-high heat, heat the oil. Add the garlic, pepper flakes, and anchovies and stir until fragrant, about 1 minute. Stir in the beans.

3. Pour the bean mixture over the pasta and add all the reserved cooking water. Cook over medium-high heat, stirring, until the pasta is cooked and a creamy sauce has formed. Season with salt and pepper. Serve with pecorino on the side.

Pasta with Balsamic Sausage and Peppers

Balsamic vinegar adds a hint of sweetness to this pasta.

PREP TIME: 10 MINUTES • **COOK TIME: 18 MINUTES** • **MAKES: 4 SERVINGS**

Salt
12 ounces cavatelli or orecchiette
¼ cup extra-virgin olive oil
½ pound bulk Italian pork or turkey
   sausage (spicy or mild)
1 medium red onion, cut in half and thinly
   sliced
1 tablespoon minced garlic
1 jar (12 ounces) roasted peppers, drained
   and coarsely chopped
2 tablespoons balsamic vinegar
2 tablespoons chopped Italian parsley
Freshly ground black pepper
Grated Parmesan cheese, for serving

1. In a large saucepot over high heat, bring 2 quarts of water to boiling. Add salt to taste and the pasta. Cook until almost al dente, 6 to 8 minutes. Reserve ½ cup cooking water, drain, and return pasta to the saucepot.

2. In a large skillet over medium-high heat, heat the oil. Add the sausage and cook, stirring frequently, until browned, 6 to 8 minutes. Stir in the onion and garlic and cook until softened, about 5 minutes longer. Stir in the peppers, balsamic vinegar, and parsley. Season with salt and pepper.

3. Pour the sausage mixture over the pasta, add half the cooking water, and toss until mixed, adding more cooking water if the mixture seems dry. Divide among serving dishes and serve with Parmesan on the side.

Cheesy Fusilli

For richer Cheddar flavor, substitute shredded medium-sharp Cheddar for the cheese blend.

PREP TIME: 5 MINUTES • COOK TIME: 20 MINUTES • MAKES: 4 SERVINGS

Salt
½ pound fusilli
3 tablespoons unsalted butter
2 large eggs, beaten
1 can (12 ounces) evaporated milk
Pinch cayenne pepper
½ teaspoon Dijon mustard
1 package (8 to 12 ounces) shredded
   cheese blend

1. In a large saucepot over high heat, bring 2 quarts of water to boiling. Add salt to taste and the fusilli. Cook just until the fusilli are al dente, 7 to 9 minutes. Drain the fusilli and return it to the saucepot. Add the butter and stir until melted. Reduce the heat to medium-low.

2. Meanwhile, in a large bowl, mix together the eggs, milk, cayenne, mustard, and cheese. Pour over the fusilli and stir constantly until the cheese is melted and the mixture begins to thicken, 7 to 10 minutes. (Don't let the mixture boil or it will get grainy.) Season with salt if necessary and serve immediately.

Cheesy Fusilli with Broccoli and Sausage

From-scratch cheese sauce? Once you see how easy it is, you'll never go back to boxed.

PREP TIME: 5 MINUTES • COOK TIME: 20 MINUTES • MAKES: 4 SERVINGS

Salt
½ pound fusilli
1 cup fresh broccoli florets
3 tablespoons unsalted butter
1 tablespoon olive oil
1 fresh Italian sausage (either spicy or
    sweet, 3 to 4 ounces total), cut into
    ½-inch rounds
2 large eggs, beaten
1 can (12 ounces) evaporated milk
Pinch cayenne pepper
½ teaspoon Dijon mustard
1 package (8 to 12 ounces) shredded
    cheese blend

1. In a large saucepot over high heat, bring 2 quarts of water to boiling. Add salt to taste and the fusilli. When the fusilli has cooked for 5 minutes, stir in the broccoli.

Cook until both are cooked through, about 3 minutes longer. Drain and return the fusilli and broccoli to the saucepot. Add the butter and stir until melted. Reduce the heat to medium-low.

2. Meanwhile, in a small nonstick skillet over medium-high heat, heat the olive oil. Add sausage and cook, stirring frequently, until browned and cooked through, 5 to 8 minutes. Remove sausage with a slotted spoon and stir into the fusilli mixture.

3. In a large bowl, combine the eggs, milk, cayenne, mustard, and cheese. Stir until mixed. Pour mixture over the fusilli and stir until the cheese is melted and the sauce begins to thicken, 7 to 10 minutes. (Don't let the mixture boil or it will get grainy.) Season with salt if necessary and serve immediately.

Fusilli with Red Peppers, Bacon, and Potatoes

Use the largest skillet you have for this dish—you'll need plenty of space for the pasta to cook.

PREP TIME: 10 MINUTES • COOK TIME: 25 MINUTES • MAKES: 4 SERVINGS

6 strips bacon
2 tablespoons extra-virgin olive oil
1 tablespoon minced garlic
1 ½ cups peeled and diced Yukon Gold or
   Yellow Finn potatoes (about ½ pound)
1 cup chicken broth
1 jar (12 ounces) roasted red peppers,
   drained and chopped
1 can (15 ounces) chickpeas, drained
Salt
1 pound fusilli
½ cup (4 ounces) goat cheese, plus more
   for serving
2 tablespoons chopped Italian parsley
Freshly ground black pepper

1. In a large skillet over medium-high heat, cook the bacon until crisp and brown, about 5 minutes. Transfer to a paper towel-lined plate. Discard all but 2 tablespoons bacon fat. Add the olive oil and garlic to the pan and cook 30 seconds. Stir in the potatoes, broth, red peppers, and chickpeas and bring to a boil. Simmer until the potatoes are very tender, about 10 minutes.

2. In a large saucepot over high heat, bring 4 quarts of water to boiling. Add salt to taste and the fusilli. Cook until three quarters done, 5 to 6 minutes. Reserve 2 cups cooking water, drain the fusilli, and transfer it to the skillet along with 1 cup reserved cooking water. Cook, stirring, until the fusilli absorbs some of the sauce and is al dente, 2 to 3 minutes longer, adding more cooking water if the mixture seems dry. Crumble or chop the bacon and stir in along with ½ cup of goat cheese, the parsley, and additional salt and black pepper. Transfer to serving bowl, dot with additional goat cheese and serve.

Fusilli with Mushrooms and Sardines

Sardines packed in olive oil have the best flavor for this fast pasta.

PREP TIME: 10 MINUTES • **COOK TIME: 15 MINUTES** • **MAKES: 4 SERVINGS**

Salt
1 pound fusilli
1 can (3.75 ounces) brisling sardines
    packed in olive oil
3 tablespoons extra-virgin olive oil
3 packages (8 ounces each) sliced cremini
    or button mushrooms
½ cup chopped Italian parsley
1 tablespoon minced garlic
Freshly ground black pepper

1. In a large saucepot over high heat, bring 4 quarts of water to boiling. Add salt to taste and the fusilli. Cook until almost al dente, 5 to 7 minutes. Reserve 1 cup cooking water, drain the fusilli, and return it to the saucepot.

2. Drain the oil from the sardines into a large skillet over high heat. Add the olive oil to the skillet and add the mushrooms. Season with salt and cook until the mushrooms are soft and browned, 5 to 7 minutes.

3. Pour the reserved cooking water into the skillet and bring to boiling, scraping up any browned bits clinging to the bottom of the pan. Pour mushroom mixture over the pasta. Add the parsley, garlic, and sardines and toss until combined. Season with salt and pepper and serve immediately.

Pasta with Carrots, Peas, and Ham

This pasta is both smoky (from the ham) and sweet (from the carrots and peas).

PREP TIME: 10 MINUTES • COOK TIME: 10 MINUTES • MAKES: 4 TO 6 SERVINGS

Salt
1 pound farfalle
2 tablespoons unsalted butter
1 ½ cups shredded carrots
1 cup frozen baby peas
1 cup thinly sliced Black Forest ham,
   (about 4 ounces) chopped
Freshly ground black pepper
2 large eggs, beaten
2 tablespoons heavy cream
1 cup grated Parmesan cheese, plus more
   for serving

1. In a large saucepot over high heat, bring 4 quarts of water to boiling. Add salt to taste and the farfalle. Cook until al dente, 7 to 9 minutes. Drain well.

2. In a large skillet over medium-high heat, melt the butter. Add the carrots, peas, and ham and cook, stirring frequently, until vegetables are crisp-tender, 2 to 3 minutes. Season with salt and pepper.

3. Meanwhile, in a large bowl, stir together the eggs, cream, and 1 cup Parmesan. Add the drained farfalle and stir until the cheese melts and the mixture forms a sauce. Add the carrot mixture and toss until combined. Season with salt and pepper. Divide among serving dishes and serve immediately with additional Parmesan on the side.

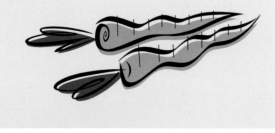

Red Pepper-Tuna Pasta

Make sure to just warm the tuna in this sauce—it's best to avoid cooking it too much.

PREP TIME: 10 MINUTES • COOK TIME: 12 MINUTES • MAKES: 4 SERVINGS

Salt
1 pound farfalle
¼ cup extra-virgin olive oil
1 red onion, halved and thinly sliced
2 medium zucchini, halved lengthwise and
   thinly sliced
1 tablespoon minced garlic
Pinch red pepper flakes
1 jar (12 ounces) roasted red peppers,
   drained and chopped
1 can (6 ounces) tuna packed in olive oil
3 tablespoons chopped parsley
Freshly ground black pepper

1. In a large saucepot over high heat, bring 4 quarts of water to boiling. Add salt to taste and the farfalle. Cook until al dente, 6 to 8 minutes. Reserve ½ cup of the cooking water. Drain well and transfer to a large serving bowl.

2. Meanwhile, in a large skillet over medium-high heat, heat the oil. Add the onion and zucchini. Sprinkle with salt and cook until soft, about 5 minutes. Stir in the garlic and pepper flakes. Cook until fragrant, about 30 seconds. Stir in the peppers, the tuna and its oil, and the parsley. Heat just until warmed through.

3. Add the tuna mixture and half the cooking water to the farfalle. Season with pepper and toss until mixed, adding more cooking water if the mixture seems dry. Serve immediately.

VARIATION

**Red Pepper-Tuna Pasta with
Olives and Lemon**
Drizzle farfalle in serving bowl with 1 tablespoon lemon-flavored avocado or olive oil. Add 1 tablespoon grated lemon zest and ½ cup pitted and chopped oil-cured or Kalamata olives to the warm tuna mixture just before adding it to the farfalle.

Linguine with Shrimp, Basil, and Lemon

Lemon-flavored avocado oil is great in this light and lemony pasta but if it's hard to find, substitute lemon-flavored olive oil.

PREP TIME: 10 MINUTES • COOK TIME: 10 MINUTES • MAKES: 4 SERVINGS

Salt
1 pound linguine
1 cup ricotta cheese
3 tablespoons heavy cream
2 tablespoons lemon-flavored avocado oil
1 tablespoon minced garlic
1 pound frozen shelled large shrimp, thawed
1 tablespoon grated lemon zest
Pinch red pepper flakes
1 cup frozen baby peas
Freshly ground black pepper
1/3 cup chopped fresh basil

1. In a large saucepot over high heat, bring 4 quarts of water to boiling. Add salt to taste and the linguine. Cook until almost al dente, 7 to 8 minutes. Reserve 1/2 cup of the cooking water and drain.

2. Meanwhile, in the bowl of a food processor with the steel blade attached, combine the ricotta and cream. Purée until smooth.

3. In a large skillet over medium-high heat, heat the lemon oil. Add the garlic and cook 30 seconds. Stir in the shrimp, lemon zest, and pepper flakes, and cook, stirring, just until shrimp are opaque, 1 to 2 minutes. Stir in the linguine, the ricotta mixture, the peas, and half the reserved cooking water. Cook, stirring, until the ricotta and peas are heated through, 1 to 2 minutes, adding more cooking water if the mixture seems dry. Season with salt and pepper, sprinkle with basil, and toss until mixed. Serve hot or warm.

Linguine with Pesto Clam Sauce

This hearty sauce is loaded with extras like potatoes and zucchini.

PREP TIME: 15 MINUTES • COOK TIME: 15 MINUTES • MAKES: 4 TO 6 SERVINGS

Salt
1 pound linguine
¼ cup extra-virgin olive oil
1 tablespoon minced garlic
Pinch hot red pepper flakes
½ pound Yukon Gold or Yellow Finn potatoes, peeled and cut into ½-inch dice
2 cans (6½ ounces each) chopped clams with juice
½ cup white wine or bottled clam juice
2 medium zucchini, diced
Freshly ground black pepper
1 jar (6 ounces) basil pesto
Grated Parmesan cheese, for serving

1. In a large saucepot over high heat, bring 4 quarts of water to boiling. Add salt to taste and the linguine. Cook until al dente, 7 to 9 minutes. Drain and return to the saucepot.

2. In a large skillet over medium-high heat, heat the oil. Add the garlic and pepper flakes and cook 1 minute. Stir in the potatoes, the clams and their juices, and the wine or clam juice. Bring to boiling. Reduce heat to medium and simmer until the potatoes are cooked through, 6 to 8 minutes. Stir in the zucchini and simmer until the zucchini are tender, 2 to 3 minutes longer.

3. Pour the clam mixture over the linguine and toss until combined. Season with salt and pepper. Divide among serving dishes. Spoon 1 tablespoon of pesto onto each and serve with the grated Parmesan and remaining pesto on the side.

Linguine with Arugula and Goat Cheese Pesto

If you're not a fan of goat cheese, you can substitute 2 cups of grated Parmesan in this bright green pesto.

PREP TIME: 10 MINUTES • COOK TIME: 10 MINUTES • MAKES: 4 SERVINGS

Salt
1 pound linguine
2 tablespoons walnut halves or pieces
2 packed cups (about 3 ounces) prewashed arugula
2 cloves garlic, peeled
¼ cup extra-virgin olive oil
Freshly ground black pepper
1 cup (8 ounces) fresh goat cheese

1. In a large saucepot over high heat, bring 4 quarts of water to boiling. Add salt to taste and the linguine. Cook until al dente, 8 to 10 minutes. Drain the linguine and transfer it to a large serving bowl.

2. Meanwhile, in the bowl of a food processor with the steel blade attached, combine the walnuts, arugula, and garlic. Process until finely chopped. With the motor running, add in the olive oil, pouring in a steady stream. Add a large pinch each of salt and pepper and half the goat cheese and pulse until combined.

3. Add the pesto to the linguine and toss until linguine is coated. Dot with the remaining goat cheese and serve.

VARIATION

Linguine with Arugula-Goat Cheese Pesto and Plum Tomatoes
Just before serving, sprinkle 2 chopped plum tomatoes over the pasta in serving bowl.

Lima Beans, Pancetta, and Linguine

For lovers of limas, this is wonderful comfort food, rich, subtle, and a pleasure to eat.

PREP TIME: 5 MINUTES • COOK TIME: 15 MINUTES • MAKES: 4 SERVINGS

Salt
12 ounces fresh linguine
2 tablespoons extra-virgin olive oil
½ cup chopped pancetta (about 4 ounces)
1 package (10 ounces) frozen baby lima
  beans
½ cup chicken broth
½ cup heavy cream
Freshly ground black pepper
½ cup grated Parmesan cheese, plus more
  for serving

1. In a large saucepot over high heat, bring 2 quarts of water to boiling. Add salt to taste and the linguine. Cook until almost al dente, about 2 minutes. Drain well.

2. Meanwhile, in a large skillet over medium-high heat, heat the olive oil. Add the pancetta and cook until crisp and brown, about 5 minutes. Using a slotted spoon, remove the pancetta to a paper towel-lined plate. Add the lima beans, broth, and cream to the skillet. Cover, reduce heat to medium, and simmer until the beans are cooked through, 5 to 6 minutes. Season with salt.

3. Add linguine to the skillet. Toss until the linguine absorbs some of the sauce, about 2 minutes. Season with salt and pepper, add ½ cup of Parmesan, and toss until mixed. Divide among serving dishes and serve with additional Parmesan on the side.

Chili-Oil Linguine with Pork

I used hot-chili sesame oil, but you can use whatever Chinese-style hot pepper oil you prefer.

PREP TIME: 5 MINUTES • COOK TIME: 15 MINUTES • MAKES: 4 SERVINGS

Salt
1 pound fresh linguine
1 tablespoon canola or vegetable oil
1 pound boneless pork shoulder, cut into
   1-inch-thick strips
5 teaspoons Chinese-style hot chili oil
Freshly ground black pepper
2 tablespoons minced garlic
1 package (8 ounces) sliced mushrooms
2 tablespoons soy sauce, plus more for
   serving
1 tablespoon Thai fish sauce
½ cup shredded basil

1. In a large saucepot over high heat, bring 4 quarts of water to boiling. Add salt to taste and the linguine. Cook just until al dente, 3 to 5 minutes. Drain the linguine and return it to the saucepot.

2. In a large nonstick skillet over medium-high heat, heat the canola oil. In a medium bowl, toss the pork with 2 teaspoons chili oil and sprinkle with salt and pepper. Add the pork to the skillet and cook until brown and cooked through, about 8 minutes. Transfer pork to a plate and cover with foil to keep warm.

3. In the same skillet over medium-high heat, heat the remaining 3 teaspoons chili oil. Add the garlic and mushrooms. Cook until soft, stirring frequently, 3 to 5 minutes. Stir in the linguine, soy sauce, fish sauce, and basil. Divide among serving dishes, top each with pork, and serve immediately.

VARIATION

Chili-Oil Linguine with Chicken
Substitute 4 boneless, skinless chicken breast halves for the pork. Brush with 2 teaspoons chili oil and cook, turning once, until just cooked through, 3 to 4 minutes per side. Continue as directed above. Top each serving with one chicken breast.

Artichoke Sauce over Fettuccine

I like to use pancetta in this dish, but if it's unavailable, substitute 4 strips of thick-cut bacon.

PREP TIME: 10 MINUTES • COOK TIME: 7 MINUTES • MAKES: 4 SERVINGS

Salt
1 pound fresh fettuccine
3 tablespoons extra-virgin olive oil
4 ounces coarsely chopped pancetta
2 jars (12 ounces each) marinated
   artichoke hearts, drained and coarsely
   chopped
½ cup chopped Italian parsley
Large pinch hot red pepper flakes
1 cup shredded Parmesan cheese
Freshly ground black pepper

1. In a large saucepot over high heat, bring 4 quarts of water to boiling. Add salt to taste and the fettuccine. Cook until al dente, 3 to 4 minutes. Reserve ½ cup of the cooking water. Drain the fettuccine and return it to the saucepot.

2. Meanwhile, in a large skillet over medium-high heat, heat the olive oil. Add the pancetta and cook until crisp. Using a slotted spoon, transfer to a paper towel-lined plate. Add the artichoke hearts, parsley, and pepper flakes to the skillet and stir until warm, about 1 minute.

3. Add the artichoke mixture, half the reserved cooking water, and half the cheese to the drained fettuccine and toss to combine. Add more cooking water if the mixture seems dry. Season with salt and pepper, divide among serving dishes, and sprinkle each serving with pancetta. Serve the remaining cheese and black pepper on the side.

Two-Cheese Pasta Frittata

This frittata is perfect for entertaining since it tastes best either warm or at room temperature.

PREP TIME: 10 MINUTES • COOK TIME: 15 MINUTES • MAKES: 4 SERVINGS

2 tablespoons extra-virgin olive oil
2 ounces pancetta or two strips of bacon, chopped
3 cups cooked fettuccine
6 eggs
½ cup feta crumbles
1 plum tomato, chopped
½ cup pesto
½ cup grated Parmesan cheese
Salt and freshly ground black pepper

1. Heat the broiler. In an ovenproof 12-inch nonstick skillet over high heat, heat the oil. Add the pancetta and cook until browned and crisp, 3 to 4 minutes. Stir in the fettuccine and cook, stirring, until warmed, 2 to 3 minutes. Meanwhile, in a large bowl, beat together the eggs, feta, tomato, pesto, and the Parmesan cheese. Season with salt and pepper. Pour egg mixture over the fettuccine and cook without stirring until the bottom is set, about 4 minutes.

2. Broil the frittata 2 to 3 inches from the heat until browned and bubbling, 2 to 3 minutes. Using a spatula, loosen the bottom and sides of the frittata and slide it onto a serving platter. To serve, cut into wedges.

Portobello and Penne Frittata

You can substitute a package of sliced cremini mushrooms for the portobellos if you prefer. A salad of baby greens dressed with a light vinaigrette goes perfectly with this frittata.

PREP TIME: 5 MINUTES • COOK TIME: 15 MINUTES • MAKES: 4 SERVINGS

¼ cup plus 2 tablespoons extra-virgin olive oil

1 package (8 ounces) sliced portobello mushrooms

2 teaspoons chopped fresh rosemary

Salt and freshly ground black pepper

3 cups cooked penne (about 1 ½ cups uncooked)

8 large eggs

1 cup shredded Asiago cheese

1. Heat the broiler. In an ovenproof nonstick 12-inch skillet over medium-high heat, heat the oil. Add the mushrooms, rosemary, and salt. Cook until mushrooms are browned, stirring frequently, about 5 minutes. Season with pepper. Stir in the penne and heat until warmed through, 2 to 3 minutes.

2. Meanwhile, in a large bowl, beat together the eggs and ½ cup Asiago. Season with salt and pepper and pour over the penne. Cook, without stirring, until the bottom is set, about 4 minutes.

3. Sprinkle the frittata with the remaining ½ cup of cheese and then broil 2 to 3 inches from the heat until browned and bubbling, 2 to 3 minutes. Using a spatula, loosen the bottom and sides of the frittata and slide it onto a serving platter. To serve, cut into wedges.

Penne with Lemon, Asparagus, and Eggs

Lemon-flavored avocado oil is great in this recipe. It has a high smoking point so it doesn't burn while pan-roasting the asparagus.

PREP TIME: 5 MINUTES • COOK TIME: 15 MINUTES • MAKES: 4 SERVINGS

Salt

1 pound penne

2 tablespoons lemon-flavored avocado or olive oil

1 pound thin asparagus, trimmed and cut into 2-inch pieces

Freshly ground black pepper

3 tablespoons unsalted butter

1 teaspoon grated lemon zest

4 large eggs

½ cup grated Parmesan cheese, plus more for serving

1. In a large saucepot over high heat, bring 4 quarts of water to boiling. Add salt to taste and the penne. Cook until al dente, 7 to 9 minutes. Reserve ½ cup cooking water and drain well.

2. Meanwhile, in a large skillet over medium-high heat, heat the oil until very hot but not smoking. Add the asparagus, sprinkle with salt and pepper, and cook, stirring occasionally, until the asparagus is nearly cooked through, about 5 minutes. Add 1 tablespoon of the butter and cook 1 minute longer. Sprinkle with the lemon zest and transfer to a large bowl. Add the pasta and toss with ½ cup of the cheese. Cover with foil to keep warm.

3. In the same skillet over medium-high heat, heat the remaining 2 tablespoons of lemon oil. Break the eggs, one at a time, into the skillet and cook until the whites are set and the yolks are still runny, 4 to 6 minutes. Divide the penne mixture among 4 serving dishes and top each serving with a fried egg. Serve immediately with grated Parmesan on the side.

Penne with Smoked Turkey and Pesto

For a nice variation and to add color, dice ½ cup of red or yellow bell pepper and sprinkle on top.

PREP TIME: 5 MINUTES • COOK TIME: 10 MINUTES • MAKES: 4 SERVINGS

Salt

1 pound penne

¼ pound smoked turkey, thinly sliced
and coarsely chopped

1 bunch watercress, tough stems
removed, coarsely chopped

½ cup prepared pesto

½ cup grated Parmesan cheese, plus more
for serving

Freshly ground black pepper

1. In a large saucepot over high heat, bring 4 quarts of water to boiling. Add salt to taste and the penne. Cook until al dente, 7 to 9 minutes. Drain.

2. Meanwhile, in a large bowl, combine the turkey, watercress, pesto, and ½ cup Parmesan. Add penne, season with salt and pepper, and toss until combined. Serve with additional Parmesan on the side.

Penne with Grilled Eggplant

A gas grill makes this pasta simple and fast. If you don't have one and don't want to light up a charcoal grill, broil the eggplant in your oven.

PREP TIME: 10 MINUTES • COOK TIME: 15 MINUTES • MAKES: 4 SERVINGS

2 medium eggplant (about 12 ounces each), cut in lengthwise ½-inch slices

¼ cup plus 2 tablespoons balsamic vinegar and oil dressing

Salt and freshly ground black pepper

1 teaspoon minced garlic

½ cup pitted Kalamata olives

¼ cup chopped fresh basil

2 tablespoons chopped fresh mint

12 ounces penne

½ cup grated pecorino Romano cheese, plus more for serving

1. Heat a gas or charcoal grill. Lay the eggplant slices on a cookie sheet and brush with the ¼ cup of the balsamic dressing. Sprinkle with salt and pepper. Grill until tender and lightly browned on both sides, 3 to 4 minutes per side. Transfer to a cutting board and chop coarsely. Pour into a large serving bowl and add the garlic, olives, basil, and mint.

2. Meanwhile, in a large saucepot over high heat, bring 3 quarts of water to boiling. Add salt to taste and the penne. Cook until al dente, 7 to 9 minutes. Drain penne and add to the egglant mixture. Add the remaining 2 tablespoons of balsamic dressing and ½ cup pecorino. Season with salt and pepper and toss until combined. Serve immediately or just slightly warm with additional pecorino on the side.

Pasta with Tuna, Celery, and Capers

Here's a dish that you can make almost entirely from staples—lemon, capers, and canned tuna.

PREP TIME: 10 MINUTES • COOK TIME: 15 MINUTES • MAKES: 4 SERVINGS

Salt
½ pound spaghetti
3 tablespoons pine nuts
2 tablespoons lemon-flavored avocado oil
   or olive oil
1 tablespoon minced garlic
Pinch hot red pepper flakes
2 cups thinly sliced celery hearts
1 tablespoon capers
¼ cup coarsely chopped green olives
1 can (6 ounces) tuna
   packed in olive oil
Grated zest of 1 lemon
Freshly ground black pepper
Grated Parmesan cheese,
   for serving

1. In a large saucepot over high heat, bring 2 quarts of water to boiling. Add salt to taste and the spaghetti. Cook until al dente, 7 to 9 minutes. Reserve ½ cup of the cooking water and drain well.

2. Meanwhile, in a large skillet over high heat, toast the pine nuts until lightly browned, 3 to 4 minutes. Transfer to a bowl. In the same skillet over medium-high heat, heat the oil. Add the garlic and pepper flakes and cook 30 seconds. Stir in the celery and cook until almost tender, about 3 minutes. Stir in the capers, olives, the tuna and its oil, and the lemon zest. Season with salt and pepper. Add the spaghetti and the cooking water. Simmer, stirring, for 1 minute longer. Season with salt and pepper, if necessary. Serve with grated Parmesan on the side.

Broccoli and Cauliflower Pasta

You can find bags of precut broccoli and cauliflower in the produce section.

PREP TIME: 5 MINUTES • COOK TIME: 10 MINUTES • MAKES: 4 SERVINGS

Salt

12 ounces spaghetti

3 tablespoons pine nuts

¼ cup extra-virgin olive oil

2 teaspoons anchovy paste

Pinch red pepper flakes

½ cup chopped sun-dried tomatoes in oil

6 to 7 cups cauliflower and broccoli florets (1½ pounds)

Pinch saffron threads

3 tablespoons dried currants

Freshly ground black pepper

Grated pecorino Romano, for serving

1. In a large saucepot over high heat, bring 3 quarts of water to boiling. Add salt to taste and the spaghetti. Cook until almost al dente, 4 to 5 minutes. Reserve ½ cup cooking water and drain.

2. Meanwhile, in a large skillet over medium-high heat, toast the pine nuts until lightly browned, about 5 minutes. Transfer to a bowl.

3. In the same skillet over medium-high heat, heat the oil. Add the anchovy paste and the pepper flakes. Cook until fragrant, about 30 seconds, then add the sun-dried tomatoes, cauliflower, and broccoli. Add 1 cup water, the saffron, currants and season with salt. Reduce heat to medium. Cover and simmer until the cauliflower and broccoli are very tender, 6 to 8 minutes.

4. Add the spaghetti and half the cooking water to the skillet. Simmer, stirring, until the spaghetti is cooked through and coated in the sauce, 2 to 3 minutes, adding more water if the mixture seems dry. Stir in the pine nuts, sprinkle with pepper and pecorino, and serve.

Spaghetti with Pecorino, Herbs, and Pepper

To make this simple but flavorful dish, you'll need very finely grated pecorino for a smooth sauce. Otherwise, the cheese tends to clump up a bit (which won't affect the flavor).

PREP TIME: 5 MINUTES • COOK TIME: 10 MINUTES • MAKES: 4 SERVINGS

Salt
1 pound spaghetti
1 cup finely grated pecorino Romano
  cheese
3 tablespoons heavy cream
2 tablespoons chopped Italian parsley
2 tablespoons chopped basil
2 tablespoons chopped mint
Freshly ground black pepper

1. In a large saucepot over high heat, bring 4 quarts of water to boiling. Add salt to taste and the spaghetti. Cook until al dente, 7 to 9 minutes. Reserve ½ cup of the cooking water and drain.

2. Pour the drained spaghetti back into the pot along with half of the reserved cooking water. Stir vigorously, sprinkling with ¾ cup pof the cheese and all the cream, and tossing in the herbs and pepper while stirring. Season with salt and toss with the remaining ¼ cup of cheese. Serve immediately.

Spaghetti Carbonara with Peas

A tomato salad would be a good partner with this rich pasta. Just slice or quarter a few tomatoes, sprinkle them with salt, pepper, vinegar, and olive oil, and serve.

PREP TIME: 5 MINUTES • COOK TIME: 10 MINUTES • MAKES: 4 SERVINGS

Salt
1 pound spaghetti
1½ cups frozen baby peas
1 tablespoon extra-virgin olive oil
3 ounces pancetta or 4 thick slices bacon, coarsely chopped
4 large eggs
½ cup grated pecorino Romano cheese
Freshly ground black pepper

1. In a large saucepot over high heat, bring 4 quarts of water to boiling. Add salt to taste and the spaghetti. Cook until the spaghetti is still al dente, 7 to 9 minutes. Add the peas and drain well.

2. Meanwhile, in a large skillet over medium-high heat, heat the oil. Add the pancetta and cook until crisp, about 5 minutes. Set aside. In a large bowl, beat the eggs and cheese together.

3. Add the hot spaghetti to the egg mixture and toss until coated. Add the pancetta, season with salt and pepper, and serve.

VARIATION

Spaghetti Carbonara with Peas and Mint
Add 2 tablespoons coarsely chopped fresh mint to the egg mixture.

Salmon Pasta with Onions and Capers

Canned salmon is great with the combination of sweet onions and salty capers. Smoked salmon or trout would be terrific as well—just use about a cup.

PREP TIME: 10 MINUTES • COOK TIME: 20 MINUTES • MAKES: 4 SERVINGS

Salt
12 ounces spaghetti
¼ cup extra-virgin olive oil
2 large red onions (about 12 ounces each), cut in half and thinly sliced
½ teaspoon sugar
Pinch red pepper flakes
2 tablespoons capers
1 can (7.5 ounces) red salmon, drained
¼ cup chopped Italian parsley
Freshly ground black pepper

1. In a large saucepot over high heat, bring 3 quarts of water to boiling. Add salt to taste and the spaghetti Cook until al dente, 7 to 9 minutes. Reserve ½ cup of cooking water and drain. Transfer to a serving bowl.

2. Meanwhile, in a large skillet over medium-high heat, heat the oil. Add the onions, a pinch of salt, the sugar, and the pepper flakes. Cook, stirring frequently, until very soft, about 10 minutes. Stir in the capers, salmon, and parsley and season with more salt and black pepper. Add the salmon mixture and half the cooking water to the pasta and toss until combined, adding more cooking water if the mixture seems dry. Serve immediately.

Pasta and Tomatoes

Linguine with Red Clam and Chorizo Sauce

When you buy fresh clams from a reliable fishmonger, there's a good chance they'll be fairly clean. Just give them a quick scrub with cold water.

PREP TIME: 10 MINUTES • COOK TIME: 20 MINUTES • MAKES: 4 SERVINGS

2 tablespoons extra-virgin olive oil
½ pound chorizo, sliced into ½-inch
   rounds
1½ tablespoons minced garlic
½ cup white wine
1 jar (18 ounces) tomato pasta sauce
3 to 4 dozen small littleneck or Manila
   clams (about 2 pounds)
Salt and freshly ground black pepper
1 pound linguine
2 tablespoons chopped
   Italian parsley,
   for garnish

1. In a large skillet over high heat, heat the oil. Add the chorizo and cook until brown on both sides, 5 to 6 minutes. Stir in the garlic and cook 30 seconds. Pour in the wine, scrape up any browned bits on the bottom, and simmer until reduced, 2 to 3 minutes. Stir in the tomato sauce and the clams, cover, and simmer, stirring occasionally, until clams have opened, 5 to 8 minutes. Season with salt and pepper.

2. Meanwhile, in a large saucepot over high heat, bring 4 quarts of water to boiling. Add salt to taste and the linguine and cook until al dente, 7 to 9 minutes. Drain well and divide among serving dishes.

3. Spoon sauce over linguine and top with clams. Sprinkle with parsley and serve.

Wagon Wheels with Sausage, Lentils, and Tomatoes

You can substitute 1 cup canned red beans for the lentils. Just freeze the remaining beans for the next time you make this sauce.

PREP TIME: 5 MINUTES • COOK TIME: 20 MINUTES • MAKES: 4 TO 6 SERVINGS

Salt
1 pound wagon wheel pasta
2 tablespoons extra-virgin olive oil
12 ounces spicy or mild Italian sausage, sliced into ¾-inch rounds
1 can (28 ounces) diced Italian tomatoes
1 cup canned cooked lentils
¼ cup chopped Italian parsley
Freshly ground black pepper
½ cup grated Parmesan cheese, for garnish

1. In a large saucepot over high heat, bring 4 quarts of water to boiling. Add salt to taste and the pasta and cook until al dente, 7 to 9 minutes. Drain well and transfer to serving dishes.

2. Meanwhile, in a large skillet over high heat, heat the oil. Add sausage and cook, stirring frequently, until browned, 5 to 6 minutes. Stir in the tomatoes and simmer 5 minutes. Stir in the lentils and simmer 2 minutes longer. Stir in the parsley and season with salt and pepper. Spoon sauce over pasta, sprinkle with Parmesan, and serve.

Pasta with Ricotta, Greens, and Tomatoes

You can substitute 1 bunch of coarsely chopped fresh spinach or Swiss chard for the spinach.

PREP TIME: 5 MINUTES • COOK TIME: 10 MINUTES • MAKES: 4 SERVINGS

Salt
12 ounces farfalle
½ pound prewashed spinach
¼ cup extra-virgin olive oil
2 tablespoon minced garlic
1½ cups canned diced tomatoes
1 teaspoon sugar
¾ cup whole milk ricotta
½ cup grated Parmesan cheese, plus more
   for serving
Freshly ground black pepper

1. In a large saucepot over high heat, bring 2 quarts of water to boiling. Add salt to taste and the farfalle. Cook until about three-quarters cooked, 5 to 7 minutes. Add the spinach and stir just until wilted. Reserve 1 cup cooking water and drain.

2. Meanwhile, in a large skillet over medium-high heat, heat the oil. Add the garlic and cook 30 seconds. Stir in the tomatoes and sugar. Season with salt and simmer 3 minutes. Add spinach mixture and ½ cup cooking water. Cook over high heat, stirring, until the sauce coats the farfalle and the farfalle is cooked through. Add the ricotta and Parmesan and stir until warmed through. Serve with additional Parmesan and black pepper on the side.

VARIATION

Pasta with Ricotta, Greens, and Cumin-Currant-Flavored Tomatoes
Stir ½ teaspoon ground cumin and 3 tablespoons currants into the tomatoes before adding them to the skillet. Continue as directed above.

Penne with Calabrian-Inspired Sauce

If you're not a fan of marinated mushrooms, feel free to substitute another jar of artichoke hearts.

PREP TIME: 10 MINUTES • COOK TIME: 15 MINUTES • MAKES: 4 SERVINGS

Salt

1 pound penne

¼ cup extra-virgin olive oil

1 tablespoon minced garlic

Pinch red pepper flakes

1 can (28 ounces) diced tomatoes

1 teaspoon sugar

1 jar (6.5 ounces) marinated mushrooms, drained and coarsely chopped

1 jar (12 ounces) marinated artichoke hearts, drained and coarsely chopped

Freshly ground black pepper

⅓ cup chopped prosciutto (about 2 ounces) or Black Forest ham

2 tablespoons chopped Italian parsley

½ cup grated Parmesan cheese

1. In a large saucepot over high heat, bring 4 quarts of water to boiling. Add salt to taste and the penne. Cook until al dente, 7 to 9 minutes. Drain well and transfer to a large serving bowl.

2. Heat the oil in a large skillet over medium-high heat. Add the garlic and pepper flakes and cook 30 seconds. Stir in the tomatoes, sugar, mushrooms, and artichokes. Season with salt and pepper and cook until the liquid is slightly reduced, about 5 minutes. Stir in the prosciutto and parsley. Pour the sauce over the pasta, add the Parmesan, and toss until mixed. Serve immediately.

Steak Pizzaiola with Penne

Top round, tri-tip, or ribeye will all work for this recipe. If you buy 1-inch-thick steaks, slice them in half crosswise. Stand back when you pour in the red wine—it will spatter.

PREP TIME: 5 MINUTES • COOK TIME: 20 MINUTES • MAKES: 4 SERVINGS

2 pounds steak, cut ½ inch thick
Salt and freshly ground black pepper
3 tablespoons extra-virgin olive oil
1 pound penne
6 cloves garlic, peeled and lightly crushed
Pinch red pepper flakes
½ cup red wine
1 can (28 ounces) diced Italian tomatoes
1 teaspoon sugar
1 bay leaf
6 to 8 basil leaves, coarsely chopped

1. Season the meat on both sides with salt and pepper. Heat a 12-inch skillet over high heat for 1 minute. Add 1 tablespoon oil and as many pieces of steak as will fit without crowding the skillet. Sear the steaks until browned, turning once, about 8 minutes for medium-rare. Transfer steaks to a plate. Repeat with 1 tablespoon oil and the remaining steaks.

2. Meanwhile, in a large saucepot over high heat, bring 4 quarts of water to boiling. Add salt to taste and the penne. Cook until al dente, 7 to 9 minutes, and drain.

3. In the same skillet over medium-high heat, heat the remaining tablespoon oil. Add the garlic and pepper flakes and cook, using a wooden spoon to mash the garlic until the garlic is browned, 1 to 2 minutes. Carefully add the red wine. Simmer, scraping up the browned bits on the bottom, until a thick glaze forms, 2 to 3 minutes. Stir in the tomatoes, sugar, and bay leaf. Season with salt and pepper. Bring to simmering and cook 5 minutes. Return the steaks and any juices that have collected to the pan. Cook 1 minute longer. Remove bay leaf.

4. Divide penne among serving dishes. Top each with sauce, then a steak. Sprinkle with basil and serve immediately.

Fusilli with Chicken and Roasted Red Pepper Sauce

If the bacon seems very fatty, you can omit the olive oil from the recipe.

PREP TIME: 5 MINUTES • COOK TIME: 45 MINUTES • MAKES: 4 SERVINGS

Salt
1 pound fusilli
4 strips thick-cut bacon, about 4 ounces
2 tablespoons extra-virgin olive oil
8 chicken drumsticks
Freshly ground black pepper
½ cup dry white wine
1 can (28 ounces) diced tomatoes
1 jar (12 ounces) roasted red and yellow
    peppers with garlic, drained and
    coarsely chopped
2 tablespoons chopped Italian parsley
½ cup grated Parmesan cheese

1. In a large saucepot over high heat, bring 4 quarts of water to boiling. Add salt to taste and the fusilli and cook until al dente, 7 to 9 minutes. Drain well and transfer to a large serving bowl.

2. Meanwhile, in a large skillet over medium-high heat, cook the bacon in the olive oil until browned and crisp, about 8 minutes. Transfer bacon to a paper towel-lined plate. Sprinkle the drumsticks generously with salt and pepper and cook in the same skillet until browned on all sides, 4 to 6 minutes. Stir in the wine, scrape up all the browned bits on the bottom of the skillet, and simmer 1 minute. Stir in the tomatoes and peppers. Cover and simmer until drumsticks are cooked through, 15 to 20 minutes longer. Season sauce with salt and pepper. Coarsely chop the bacon and add it and the parsley to the pan.

3. Transfer the drumsticks to a plate. Pour the sauce over the fusilli. Add Parmesan and toss until mixed. Arrange the drumsticks on top of the fusilli. Serve immediately.

Rigatoni with White Beans and Herbs

This pasta gets loads of fresh flavor from chopped fresh parsley, basil, and mint. When you purchase the parsley, make sure to buy flat-leaf Italian variety, not curly leaf parsley.

PREP TIME: 5 MINUTES • COOK TIME: 15 MINUTES • MAKES: 4 SERVINGS

Salt
1 pound rigatoni
¼ cup extra-virgin olive oil
1 tablespoon minced garlic
Pinch hot red pepper flakes
1 can (15 ounces) white beans, drained
   and rinsed
1 teaspoon sugar
1 can (28 ounces) diced Italian tomatoes
2 tablespoons chopped Italian parsley
2 tablespoons chopped basil
2 tablespoons chopped fresh mint
Freshly ground black pepper
½ cup grated Parmesan cheese, for
   garnish

1. In a large saucepot over high heat, bring 4 quarts of water to boiling. Add salt to taste and the rigatoni and cook until al dente, 7 to 9 minutes. Drain well and transfer to serving dishes.

2. In a large skillet over medium-high heat, heat the oil. Add garlic, pepper flakes, and beans. Cook 1 minute. Stir in the sugar and tomatoes and bring to boiling. Reduce heat to medium and simmer 5 minutes. Stir in the parsley, basil, and mint. Season with salt and pepper. Spoon sauce over rigatoni. Sprinkle with Parmesan and serve.

Sausage, Cream, and Tomato Pasta

This is a fantastic pasta dish, rustic but very rich and flavorful. Make a simple green salad to accompany it and get a good loaf of crusty bread to sop up the sauce.

PREP TIME: 5 MINUTES • COOK TIME: 35 MINUTES • MAKES: 4 TO 6 SERVINGS

2 tablespoons extra-virgin olive oil
1 pound mild Italian sausage, sliced into
  ½-inch rounds
1 medium yellow onion, finely chopped
Pinch ground cloves
1 bay leaf
1 cup dry white wine
1 can (28 ounces) diced Italian tomatoes
½ cup heavy cream
Salt
1 pound ziti
½ cup grated Parmesan cheese, plus more
  for serving

1. In a large skillet over medium-high heat, heat the oil. Add the sausage and cook, stirring, until browned and cooked through, 5 to 6 minutes. Transfer to a bowl. Add the onion to the pan. Cook until very soft, about 5 minutes. Stir in the cloves, bay leaf, and the wine. Simmer until the wine is almost completely evaporated, 6 to 8 minutes, stirring occasionally. Stir in the sausage, tomatoes, and cream and simmer until slightly thickened, about 10 minutes.

2. Meanwhile, in a large saucepot over high heat, bring 2 quarts of water to boiling. Add salt to taste and the ziti. Cook until al dente, 7 to 9 minutes. Drain well and pour into a large serving dish. Remove the bay leaf from the sauce and spoon the sauce over. Sprinkle with ½ cup Parmesan and toss until mixed. Serve with additional Parmesan on the side.

Pasta with Chicken, Green Olives, and Red Sauce

If you prefer to use 4 boneless, skinless chicken breasts, just brown them on both sides and simmer for 5 minutes in the sauce.

PREP TIME: 5 MINUTES • COOK TIME: 50 MINUTES • MAKES: 4 SERVINGS

8 boneless, skinless chicken thighs (about 2 pounds)
Salt and freshly ground black pepper
2 tablespoons lemon-flavored avocado or olive oil
1 large sweet onion (such as Walla Walla or Vidalia), cut in half and thinly sliced
1 cup white wine
2 cups jarred marinara sauce
½ cup green olives, pitted and chopped
1 teaspoon grated lemon zest
1 pound rigatoni

1. Sprinkle both sides of the chicken with salt and pepper. Heat a 12-inch nonstick skillet over high heat for 1 minute. Add 1 tablespoon oil and half the chicken. Cook, turning once, until browned, 6 to 7 minutes.

Transfer to a plate. Repeat with the remaining oil and chicken. Add the onion and wine, scraping up any browned bits on the bottom of the pan. Simmer until the wine is evaporated and the onion is lightly browned and soft, about 10 minutes. Stir in the marinara sauce and return the chicken and any juices that have collected to the skillet. Stir in the olives and lemon zest. Cover and simmer until the chicken is cooked through, about 15 minutes.

2. Meanwhile, in a large saucepot over high heat, bring 2 quarts of water to boiling. Add salt to taste and the rigatoni. Cook until al dente, 7 to 9 minutes, drain well, and return to the saucepot. Transfer the chicken to a plate. Spoon the sauce over the rigatoni; toss. Divide the mixture among serving dishes and top each with two pieces of chicken. Serve immediately.

Fettuccine with Pesto, Tomatoes, and Salmon

Use pliers to remove the tiny pin bones from the salmon fillet if your fishmonger has not removed them already.

PREP TIME: 10 MINUTES • COOK TIME: 15 MINUTES • MAKES: 4 SERVINGS

Salt
1 pound fettuccine
1 cup pesto
½ cup grated Parmesan cheese, plus more
    for serving
1 tablespoon canola or grapeseed oil
¾ pound skin-on salmon fillet (about
    1 inch thick)
Freshly ground black pepper
4 plum tomatoes, cored and diced

1. In a large saucepot over high heat, bring 4 quarts of water to boiling. Add salt to taste and the fettuccine and cook until al dente, 7 to 9 minutes. Drain well and transfer to a large serving bowl. Toss with the pesto and ½ cup of Parmesan, cover, and keep warm.

2. Meanwhile, in a medium nonstick skillet over high heat, heat the oil until very hot but not smoking. Sprinkle both sides of the salmon with salt and pepper and cook, flesh-side down, 5 minutes. Turn and cook until opaque, about 3 minutes longer. Transfer to a cutting board and remove the skin. Coarsely chop the salmon. Sprinkle the salmon and diced tomatoes over the fettuccine. Toss until mixed and serve immediately with additional cheese on the side.

Rigatoni with Chickpeas and Herbed Cheese

You'll have cheese left over after you've made this dish—it's great in sandwiches or omelettes.

PREP TIME: 5 MINUTES • COOK TIME: 10 MINUTES • MAKES: 4 SERVINGS

Salt
1 pound rigatoni
¼ cup extra virgin olive oil
1 tablespoon minced garlic
Pinch red pepper flakes
1 teaspoon sugar
1 can (28 ounces) diced tomatoes
1 cup canned chickpeas, drained
¼ cup herbed cheese, plus more for
    serving
2 tablespoons chopped Italian parsley
Freshly ground black pepper

1. In a large saucepot over high heat, bring 4 quarts of water to boiling. Add salt to taste and the rigatoni and cook until al dente, 7 to 9 minutes. Drain well and transfer to serving dishes.

2. Meanwhile, in a large skillet over medium-high heat, heat the oil. Add the garlic and pepper flakes and cook 30 seconds. Stir in tomatoes and sugar and simmer 5 minutes. Stir in the chickpeas, parsley, and ¼ cup herbed cheese and heat until warmed through. Season with salt and pepper. Spoon sauce over rigatoni and top each serving with a dollop of cheese.

Easy Spaghetti Puttanesca

Jarred puttanesca just can't compare to this fast sauce. If you like anchovies, use the full amount. If you're not a big fan, just use four.

PREP TIME: 5 MINUTES • COOK TIME: 10 MINUTES • MAKES: 4 SERVINGS

Salt
1 pound spaghetti
3 tablespoons extra-virgin olive oil
2 tablespoons minced garlic
¼ teaspoon red pepper flakes
4 to 6 anchovy fillets
2 cups tomato pasta sauce
2 tablespoons capers
½ cup coarsely chopped pitted Kalamata
   olives
Freshly ground black pepper
Grated pecorino Romano cheese, for
   garnish

1. In a large saucepot over high heat, bring 4 quarts of water to boiling. Add salt to taste and the spaghetti. Cook until al dente, 7 to 9 minutes. Drain the spaghetti and divide among serving dishes.

2. Meanwhile, in a large skillet over medium high heat, heat the oil. Add the garlic, pepper flakes, and anchovies and cook, mashing and stirring until anchovies dissolve, about 1 minute. Stir in the tomato sauce, capers, and olives and bring to simmering. Season with salt and pepper. Spoon sauce over spaghetti and sprinkle with pecorino. Serve immediately.

Spaghetti with Basic Tomato Sauce

This fast sauce is fresher-tasting than any jarred sauce and it only takes 10 minutes.

PREP TIME: 5 MINUTES • COOK TIME: 20 MINUTES • MAKES: 4 SERVINGS

Salt
1 pound spaghetti
3 tablespoons extra-virgin olive oil
1 tablespoon minced garlic
Pinch red pepper flakes
1 can (28 ounces) diced tomatoes
1 teaspoon sugar
Freshly ground black pepper
Grated pecorino Romano, for serving

1. In a large saucepot over high heat, bring 4 quarts of water to boiling. Add salt to taste and the spaghetti. Cook until al dente, 7 to 9 minutes. Drain well and transfer to serving dishes.

2. In a large skillet over medium-high heat, heat the oil. Add the garlic and pepper flakes and cook 30 seconds. Stir in the tomatoes and sugar. Season with salt and pepper and cook until slightly reduced, 9 to 10 minutes. Spoon sauce over the spaghetti and sprinkle with grated cheese. Serve immediately with additional pecorino on the side.

VARIATION

Spaghetti with Tomato Sauce and Hard-Cooked Eggs
Prepare recipe as directed above. While the sauce is cooking, place 8 large eggs in a small saucepan. Fill with cold water to cover by 1 inch. Over high heat, bring just to boiling. Remove from the heat, cover, and let stand 8 minutes. Drain, then fill the saucepan with cold water. Crack the eggs against the side of the saucepan and let stand in the water 5 minutes. Peel the eggs and serve whole, 2 per serving. Let each diner chop the eggs over the spaghetti.

Spaghetti with Poached Eggs and Fennel-Tomato Sauce

Serve a sliced crusty loaf alongside to sop up every bit of the fennel-scented sauce.

PREP TIME: 5 MINUTES • COOK TIME: 25 MINUTES • MAKES: 4 SERVINGS

Salt
1 pound spaghetti
3 tablespoons extra-virgin olive oil
1 tablespoon minced garlic
½ teaspoon fennel seeds
Pinch red pepper flakes
1 can (28 ounces) diced Italian tomatoes
1 teaspoon sugar
Freshly ground black pepper
4 eggs
Grated Parmesan cheese, for serving

1. In a large saucepot over high heat, bring 4 quarts of water to boiling. Add salt to taste and the spaghetti. Cook until al dente, 7 to 9 minutes. Drain and divide among serving dishes

2. Meanwhile, in a large skillet over medium-high heat, heat the oil. Add the garlic, fennel, and pepper flakes and cook 30 seconds. Stir in the tomatoes and sugar. Season with salt and pepper and cook until slightly reduced, 9 to 10 minutes. Carefully break the eggs into the sauce, cover, and poach until cooked through, 6 to 8 minutes.

3. Spoon sauce over each serving, then top each serving with an egg and sprinkle with grated Parmesan. Serve immediately with additional Parmesan on the side.

Spaghetti with Tomato-Almond Sauce

Make the prep for this Sicilian-inspired sauce super-easy by pulsing the almonds in the food processor just until they are chopped.

PREP TIME: 10 MINUTES • COOK TIME: 10 MINUTES • MAKES: 4 SERVINGS

Salt
1 pound spaghetti
¼ cup extra-virgin olive oil
1 tablespoon minced garlic
½ cup coarsely chopped almonds
1 can (28 ounces) diced Italian tomatoes
Freshly ground black pepper
Zest of 1 large lemon

1. In a large saucepot over high heat, bring 4 quarts of water to boiling. Add salt to taste and the spaghetti. Cook until al dente, 7 to 9 minutes. Drain well.

2. Meanwhile, in a large skillet over medium-high heat, heat the oil. Add the garlic and almonds and cook 1 minute, stirring. Stir in the tomatoes. Season with salt and pepper and simmer 2 to 3 minutes. Stir in the lemon zest. Add the spaghetti to the tomato mixture. Toss until mixed and serve.

Pasta with Sun-Dried Tomatoes and Cauliflower

Most supermarkets carry sun-dried tomato pesto, but you can substitute ½ cup finely chopped sun-dried tomatoes in oil instead.

PREP TIME: 5 MINUTES • COOK TIME: 15 MINUTES • MAKES: 4 SERVINGS

Salt
1 pound fusilli or orecchiette
2 tablespoons extra-virgin olive oil
1½ tablespoons minced garlic
½ teaspoon curry powder
Pinch red pepper flakes
Pinch ground ginger
1 bag (16 ounces) frozen cauliflower florets
1 can (28 ounces) diced Italian tomatoes
½ cup sun-dried tomato pesto
Freshly ground black pepper
Feta cheese crumbles, for serving
2 tablespoons chopped cilantro or Italian parsley, for serving

1. In a large saucepot over high heat, bring 4 quarts of water to boiling. Add salt to taste and the pasta. Cook until al dente, 7 to 9 minutes. Drain well and transfer the pasta to a large bowl.

2. Meanwhile, in a large skillet over medium-high heat, heat the oil. Add the garlic, curry powder, pepper flakes, and ginger and cook 30 seconds. Add the cauliflower, tomatoes, and tomato pesto and bring to a simmer. Cover and simmer 5 minutes; uncover and continue cooking until the cauliflower is tender, 3 to 4 minutes longer. Season with salt and pepper. Pour the sauce over the pasta. Sprinkle with the feta and cilantro and serve immediately.

Shells with Sun-Dried Tomatoes and Lamb

This sauce is perfect for a quick Greek-inspired dinner. Serve with jarred stuffed grape leaves and a romaine lettuce salad.

PREP TIME: 5 MINUTES • COOK TIME: 10 MINUTES • MAKES: 4 SERVINGS

Salt
1 pound large shells
2 tablespoons extra-virgin olive oil
1 tablespoon minced garlic
Pinch red pepper flakes
1 pound ground lamb
Freshly ground black pepper
¼ cup chopped sun-dried tomatoes in oil
1 can (28 ounces) diced tomatoes
½ teaspoon dried oregano
Feta cheese crumbles, for serving

1. In a large saucepot over high heat, bring 4 quarts of water to boiling. Add salt to taste and the shells and cook until al dente, 7 to 9 minutes. Drain well and transfer to serving dishes.

2. Meanwhile, in a large skillet over medium-high heat, heat the oil. Add the garlic and pepper flakes and cook 30 seconds. Add the lamb. Season with salt and pepper and cook until browned, stirring frequently, 3 to 4 minutes. Stir in the sun-dried tomatoes, the diced tomatoes, and the oregano. Season with salt and pepper and simmer until slightly thickened, 5 to 6 minutes longer. Spoon sauce over shells, sprinkle with feta, and serve.

VARIATION

Pasta with Greek Flavors
Add ½ cup chopped pitted Kalamata olives and ½ teaspoon dried mint to the tomato mixture.

Shells with Bacon, Tomatoes, and Shrimp

If you'd rather use precooked shrimp, just add the shrimp along with the basil.

PREP TIME: 5 MINUTES • **COOK TIME: 20 MINUTES** • **MAKES: 4 SERVINGS**

Salt
1 pound small shells
4 strips thick-cut bacon (about 4 ounces)
2 tablespoons extra-virgin olive oil
3 large shallots, thinly sliced (about ¾ cup)
2 cups frozen baby white corn
½ pound frozen shelled small shrimp, thawed
1 can (15 ounces) diced fire-roasted tomatoes
½ cup coarsely chopped fresh basil
Freshly ground black pepper
½ cup grated Parmesan cheese, plus more for serving

1. In a large saucepot over high heat, bring 4 quarts of water to boiling. Add salt to taste and the shells. Cook until al dente, 7 to 9 minutes. Drain.

2. Meanwhile, in a large skillet over medium-high heat, cook the bacon until browned and crisp, about 8 minutes. Transfer the bacon to a paper towel-lined plate and add the olive oil and shallots to the pan. Cook until soft, 2 to 3 minutes. Stir in the corn, shrimp, and the tomatoes and bring to boiling. Reduce heat to medium and simmer 5 minutes. Stir in the basil and season with salt and pepper.

3. Chop the bacon and stir into the sauce with ½ cup Parmesan. Add the shells, toss until mixed, and serve with additional cheese on the side.

Pasta with Tomato, Bacon, and Bean Sauce

Thickly sliced bacon works best in this hearty sauce.

PREP TIME: 10 MINUTES • COOK TIME: 30 MINUTES • MAKES: 4 TO 6 SERVINGS

3 tablespoons unsalted butter
1 medium white onion, finely chopped
½ pound thick-cut bacon, coarsely
   chopped (about 1 ½ cups)
1 cup dry white wine
1 can (15 ounces) pinto or red beans,
   drained and rinsed
1 can (28 ounces) diced Italian tomatoes
8 fresh basil leaves
Salt and freshly ground black pepper
1 pound cavatelli or orecchiette
Grated Parmesan cheese, for garnish

1. In a large skillet over medium-high heat, melt the butter. Add the onion and cook until very soft, 3 to 4 minutes. Add the bacon and cook until browned, 5 to 6 minutes. Add the wine, scraping up any browned bits on the bottom of the pan, and simmer until the wine has almost evaporated, 4 to 5 minutes. Stir in the beans, tomatoes, and basil leaves and bring to boiling. Season with salt and pepper and simmer until reduced and thickened, about 10 minutes.

2. Meanwhile, in a large saucepot over high heat, bring 4 quarts of water to boiling. Add salt to taste and the pasta. Cook until al dente, 7 to 9 minutes. Drain well and divide among serving dishes. Spoon the sauce over and sprinkle with Parmesan. Serve immediately.

Tagliatelle with Mushroom Veal Sauce

Ground turkey (preferably dark meat) makes a good substitute for the ground veal.

COOK TIME: 20 MINUTES • MAKES: 4 SERVINGS

4 tablespoons extra-virgin olive oil
1 pound ground veal
Salt and freshly ground black pepper
1 package (8 ounces) sliced cremini or
    button mushrooms
¾ cup white wine
1 cup heavy cream
1½ cups jarred tomato pasta sauce
3 sprigs fresh thyme or ½ teaspoon dried
    thyme
1 pound fresh tagliatelle or fettuccine
½ cup grated Parmesan cheese

1. In a large skillet over high heat, heat 2 tablespoons oil. Add the veal. Season with salt and pepper and cook, stirring frequently, until browned, 4 to 5 minutes. Transfer to a bowl. Add the remaining 2 tablespoons oil to the skillet. Add the mushrooms, season with salt and pepper, and cook, stirring occasionally, until browned and soft, about 5 minutes. Stir in the wine and simmer until reduced by half, 3 to 4 minutes. Stir in the veal, cream, tomato sauce, ½ cup water, and thyme; season with salt and pepper and simmer 5 to 6 minutes longer. Remove the thyme sprigs before serving.

2. Meanwhile, in a large saucepot over high heat, bring 4 quarts of water to boiling. Add salt to taste and the pasta and cook until al dente, 3 to 4 minutes. Drain and transfer to a large serving bowl. Pour the sauce over the pasta. Sprinkle with Parmesan and toss until mixed. Serve immediately.

Smoky Eggplant Sauce over Fettuccine

If you have a gas stove, you can roast the eggplant whole, sitting right on top of the burner.

PREP TIME: 5 MINUTES • COOK TIME: 30 MINUTES • MAKES: 4 SERVINGS

1 large eggplant (about 1 pound)
Salt
1 pound fettuccine
2 tablespoons extra-virgin olive oil
1 tablespoon minced garlic
¼ teaspoon red pepper flakes
½ cup white wine
2 cups fire-roasted tomato sauce
Freshly ground black pepper
2 tablespoons chopped Italian parsley
1½ cups shredded smoked mozzarella,
   plus more for serving

1. Heat the broiler. Slice the eggplant in half lengthwise. Place eggplant cut-side down on a baking sheet and broil 2 to 3 inches from the heat until the skin is blackened and very soft, about 15 minutes. Remove and set aside to cool.

2. In a large saucepot over high heat, bring 4 quarts of water to boiling. Add salt to taste and the fettuccine and cook until al dente, 7 to 9 minutes. Drain well and transfer to serving dishes.

3. Meanwhile, in a large skillet over medium-high heat, heat the oil. Add the garlic and pepper flakes and cook 30 seconds. Stir in the wine and simmer 1 minute. Stir in the tomato sauce and bring to simmering. Using a spoon, scrape the eggplant flesh from the skin onto a large cutting board. Chop coarsely and stir into the sauce. Taste and season the sauce with salt and pepper and simmer 5 minutes longer. Stir in the parsley. Spoon sauce over the fettuccine, sprinkle with the cheese, toss, and serve.

Super-Fast Meat Sauce with Fettuccine

For variety, use "meatloaf mix"—a combination of ground pork, beef, and veal.

PREP TIME: 5 MINUTES • **COOK TIME: 15 MINUTES** • **MAKES: 4 TO 6 SERVINGS**

Salt
1 pound fettuccine
2 tablespoons extra-virgin olive oil
1 tablespoon minced garlic
Pinch hot red pepper flakes
1 pound ground beef or dark-meat ground turkey
2 tablespoons heavy cream
1 jar (25.5 ounces) tomato-basil pasta sauce
2 tablespoons chopped Italian parsley
Freshly ground black pepper
Grated Parmesan cheese, for serving

1. In a large saucepot over high heat, bring 2 quarts of water to boiling. Add salt to taste and the fettuccine and cook until al dente, 7 to 9 minutes. Drain well and transfer to serving dishes.

2. Meanwhile, in a large skillet over medium-high heat, heat the oil. Add the garlic and pepper flakes. Cook 30 seconds. Add ground meat and cook until browned, stirring frequently, 5 to 6 minutes. Stir in the cream and simmer 1 minute. Stir in the pasta sauce and bring to boiling. Pour 1/4 cup of water into the pasta sauce jar, cover, shake, and add mixture to the skillet. Simmer 2 to 3 minutes longer. Stir in the parsley. Season with salt and pepper. Spoon sauce over the fettuccine. Top with Parmesan and serve.

VARIATION

Super-Fast Meat and Sausage Sauce
Prepare as directed above, using 1/2 pound ground meat and 1/2 pound bulk ground sausage.

Spaghetti with Spicy Tuna and Artichoke Sauce

Add ¼ teaspoon red pepper flakes to the sauce if you can't find "spicy" marinated artichokes.

PREP TIME: 5 MINUTES • COOK TIME: 15 MINUTES • MAKES: 4 SERVINGS

Salt

1 pound spaghetti

2 tablespoons extra-virgin olive oil

1 tablespoon minced garlic

1 can (28 ounces) fire-roasted diced tomatoes

1 teaspoon sugar

1 jar (6.5 ounces) spicy marinated artichokes, drained and coarsely chopped

Freshly ground black pepper

1 can (6 ounces) tuna packed in olive oil

1. In a large saucepot over high heat, bring 4 quarts of water to boiling. Add salt to taste and the spaghetti and cook until al dente, 7 to 9 minutes. Drain well and divide among serving dishes.

2. Meanwhile, in a large skillet over medium-high heat, heat the oil. Add the garlic and cook 30 seconds. Stir in the tomatoes, sugar, and artichokes. Season with salt and pepper and simmer 5 minutes. Stir in the tuna and its oil. Spoon the sauce over the spaghetti and serve.

Spaghetti with Tomatoes, Mascarpone, and Bacon

Mascarpone is a luxuriously rich Italian cream cheese, great in savory sauces. If you can't find it, substitute 3 tablespoons of regular (not low-fat) cream cheese and a tablespoon of heavy cream.

PREP TIME: 5 MINUTES • **COOK TIME: 20 MINUTES** • **MAKES: 4 SERVINGS**

Salt
1 pound rigatoni
6 strips thick-cut bacon
2 tablespoons extra-virgin olive oil
1 tablespoon minced garlic
Generous pinch red pepper flakes
1 can (28 ounces) diced Italian tomatoes
Freshly ground black pepper
Finely grated zest of 1 large lemon
¼ cup mascarpone
   cheese

1. In a large saucepot over high heat, bring 4 quarts of water to boiling. Add salt to taste and the rigatoni and cook until al dente, 7 to 9 minutes. Drain well and transfer to a large serving dish.

2. Cook the bacon in a large skillet over medium-high heat until brown and crisp, about 8 minutes. Transfer the bacon to a paper towel-lined plate and discard all but 2 tablespoons of fat from the pan. Stir in the olive oil, garlic, and pepper flakes and cook 30 seconds. Stir in the tomatoes and salt. Simmer 5 minutes. Season with pepper and stir in the lemon zest and mascarpone. Coarsely chop the bacon and stir into the sauce. Spoon the sauce over the rigatoni and toss until mixed. Serve immediately.

Pizzeria Pasta

Two and a half cups of jarred pasta sauce can be substituted for the sauce ingredients to make this dish even faster.

PREP TIME: 10 MINUTES • COOK TIME: 15 MINUTES • MAKES: 4 SERVINGS

Salt
1 pound spaghetti
1 can (28 ounces) diced Italian tomatoes
¼ cup extra-virgin olive oil
1 tablespoon minced garlic
Pinch red pepper flakes
1 teaspoon sugar
½ teaspoon dried marjoram
Freshly ground black pepper
1 pound fresh mozzarella, diced
½ cup sliced pepperoni, cut into thin strips
½ cup grated Parmesan cheese, plus more
   for serving

1. In a large saucepot over high heat, bring 4 quarts of water to boiling. Add salt to taste and the spaghetti. Cook until al dente, 7 to 9 minutes. Drain and transfer to a large serving bowl.

2. Meanwhile, in the bowl of a food processor with the steel blade attached, purée the tomatoes. In a large skillet over medium-high heat, heat the oil. Add the garlic and pepper flakes and cook 30 seconds. Stir in the sugar, marjoram, and tomato purée. Season with salt and pepper and simmer until thickened, 5 minutes. Add the mozzarella and pepperoni to the spaghetti and toss until mixed. Pour the sauce over, add ½ cup Parmesan, and toss again. Serve immediately with additional Parmesan on the side.

Spaghetti with Veggies

Substitute 2 chopped shallots for the onion if you like.

PREP TIME: 10 MINUTES • COOK TIME: 15 MINUTES • MAKES: 4 SERVINGS

Salt
1 pound spaghetti
1 cup baby carrots
1 stalk celery, rinsed
1 small yellow onion, peeled and quartered
¼ cup extra-virgin olive oil
Pinch red pepper flakes
Freshly ground black pepper
1 can (28 ounces) diced Italian tomatoes
2 tablespoons chopped Italian parsley
Grated Parmesan cheese

1. In a large saucepot over high heat, bring 4 quarts of water to boiling. Add salt to taste and the spaghetti. Cook until al dente, 7 to 9 minutes, and drain. Transfer to a large serving bowl.

2. Meanwhile, in the bowl of a food processor with the steel blade attached, chop the carrots until fine. With the motor running, add the celery and onion through the feed tube. Process until finely chopped.

3. In a large skillet over medium-high heat, heat the oil. Add the pepper flakes and cook 30 seconds. Stir in the chopped vegetables and salt and cook, stirring, for 3 minutes or until vegetables are crisp-tender. Stir in the tomatoes. Season with salt and pepper and simmer 5 minutes longer. Stir in the parsley. Spoon sauce over the pasta. Sprinkle with cheese and serve.

VARIATION

Fennel and Veggie Tomato Sauce
Cut 1 fennel bulb into 1-inch chunks and add to the food processor with the celery and onion. Add ½ teaspoon fennel seeds to the sauce along with the pepper flakes. Continue as directed above.

Spaghetti with Clams, Bacon, and Peppers

Use roasted red or yellow peppers or a combination in this flavorful dish.

PREP TIME: 5 MINUTES • COOK TIME: 25 MINUTES • MAKES: 4 SERVINGS

Salt
1 pound spaghetti
4 strips thick-cut bacon
2 tablespoons extra-virgin olive oil
Pinch red pepper flakes
2 tablespoons minced garlic
1 jar (12 ounces) roasted red peppers,
   drained and coarsely chopped
1 can (14. 5 ounces) diced tomatoes, with
   their juices
1 can (6.5 ounces) chopped clams
2 tablespoons
   chopped parsley

1. In a large saucepot over high heat, bring 4 quarts of water to boiling. Add salt to taste and the spaghetti. Cook until al dente, 7 to 9 minutes. Drain and return to the saucepot.

2. Meanwhile, in a large skillet over high heat, cook the bacon until crisp, about 8 minutes. Transfer bacon to a paper towel-lined plate and discard all but 1 tablespoon of fat from the skillet. Add the oil, pepper flakes, and garlic. Cook, stirring, 30 seconds, then stir in the peppers, tomatoes, and clams and their juices. Reduce the heat to medium and simmer until the liquid is slightly reduced and thickened, about 10 minutes longer.

3. Pour the clam mixture over the spaghetti, add the parsley, and toss until mixed. Chop the bacon, add to the spaghetti mixture, and toss again. Serve immediately.

Soups and Salads

Egg Drop Angel Hair Soup with Shrimp

This is great for a light lunch or the first course of a Chinese meal.

PREP TIME: 2 MINUTES • COOK TIME: 15 MINUTES • MAKES: 4 SERVINGS

4 quarter-sized slices fresh ginger
3 large cloves garlic, peeled and lightly
  crushed
1 quart chicken broth
¾ cup broken capellini
2 large eggs, lightly beaten
Salt and freshly ground black pepper
1 tablespoon soy sauce
½ pound cooked small shrimp
3 scallions, thinly sliced, for garnish

In a saucepot over high heat, combine the ginger, garlic, and broth and bring to boiling. Reduce heat to medium and simmer 5 minutes. Add the capellini and simmer until it is almost cooked through, 4 to 5 minutes. Pour eggs into a liquid measuring cup and drizzle into the soup, stirring constantly, until eggs are set, about 1 minute. Stir in the salt and pepper, soy sauce, and shrimp and cook 1 minute longer. Before serving, discard the ginger slices and garlic. To serve, ladle soup into serving bowls and garnish with scallions.

VARIATION

Egg Drop Angel Hair Soup with Chicken
Substitute 1½ cups diced cooked chicken for the shrimp.

Avgolemono Soup with Chicken and Orzo

This Greek lemon soup is so easy, you'll make it part of your regular repertoire. Just make sure it's seasoned with plenty of lemon juice and plenty of salt. Add a Caesar salad and you are set.

PREP TIME: 5 MINUTES • COOK TIME: 20 MINUTES • MAKES: 4 SERVINGS

6 cups chicken broth
½ cup orzo
2 whole eggs
1 egg yolk
⅓ cup lemon juice, plus more, if desired
Salt and freshly ground black pepper
2 cups (½ pound) diced cooked chicken
2 tablespoons minced Italian parsley, for
serving

1. In a medium saucepot over high heat, bring the chicken broth to boiling. Stir in the orzo, reduce the heat to medium-low, and simmer until al dente, about 12 minutes. Reduce the heat to low.

2. In a large bowl, beat the eggs and egg yolk with the lemon juice until light and frothy. Beating constantly, slowly pour 1 cup of the hot stock into the egg mixture. Continue to add stock until the eggs are warmed. Pour the eggs back into the soup. Add more lemon juice if needed. Season with salt and pepper. Stir in chicken and heat until warmed through, about 5 minutes. Do not let the soup simmer.

3. To serve, ladle into serving bowls and sprinkle with parsley.

VARIATION

Avgolemono Soup with Shrimp and Orzo
Substitute 2 cups cooked diced shrimp for the chicken.

Tex-Mex Chicken Soup

For a tangy twist, serve this spicy chicken soup sprinkled with crumbled feta or goat cheese.

PREP TIME: 10 MINUTES • COOK TIME: 15 MINUTES • MAKES: 6 SERVINGS

1 tablespoon canola or vegetable oil
1 large yellow onion, chopped
2 teaspoons minced garlic
½ teaspoon ground cumin
⅛ to ¼ teaspoon red pepper flakes
1 can (14.5 ounces) fire-roasted diced
   tomatoes with green chiles
4 cups chicken broth
Salt
½ cup orzo
2 cups (about 12 ounces) diced smoked
   chicken
1 cup frozen corn kernels
1 ripe avocado, peeled, halved, and diced
½ cup coarsely chopped cilantro leaves

1. In a large saucepot over medium-high heat, heat the oil. Add the onion and cook until soft, about 5 minutes. Stir in the garlic, cumin, pepper flakes, tomatoes, and broth. Season with salt and bring to boiling.

2. Stir in the orzo, reduce heat to medium-low, and simmer until almost cooked through, about 7 minutes. Stir in the chicken and corn and just heat through, about 1 minute longer. To serve, ladle into bowls and top each bowl with a sprinkle of avocado and cilantro.

Smoked Chicken Noodle Soup

Parsnips and carrots sweeten this broth, while dill and smoked chicken provide a savory balance. Smoked turkey would be a good substitute for the chicken.

PREP TIME: 10 MINUTES • COOK TIME: 15 MINUTES • MAKES: 4 SERVINGS

2 tablespoons extra-virgin olive oil

1 medium yellow onion, chopped

3 large carrots, peeled and sliced into ½-inch-thick rounds

1 large parsnip, peeled and diced into ¾-inch pieces

4 cups chicken broth

2 ounces fettuccine

2 cups (½ pound) diced smoked chicken

1 cup frozen peas

2 tablespoons chopped dill

Salt and freshly ground black pepper

In a large saucepot, heat the oil over medium heat. Add the onion and cook until soft, 3 to 4 minutes. Add the carrots, parsnip, and broth and bring to boiling. Stir in the fettuccine, reduce heat to medium-low, and simmer, stirring occasionally, until the vegetables are soft and fettuccine is cooked, 7 to 9 minutes. Stir in the chicken, peas, and dill. Season with salt and pepper and serve.

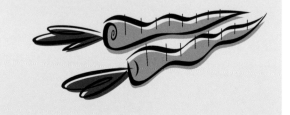

Asian Chicken Noodle Soup

You won't need takeout when you know how to make this soup. For added color, garnish with sprigs of cilantro or Thai basil.

PREP TIME: 5 MINUTES • COOK TIME: 10 MINUTES • MAKES: 4 SERVINGS

2 tablespoons peanut oil
2 shallots, thinly sliced
4 quarter-sized slices of fresh ginger
4 cups chicken broth
2 ounces rice noodles (fettuccine size)
1 cup fresh snow peas, cut into 1-inch
   pieces
2 scallions, thinly sliced
2 cups diced cooked chicken
Salt and freshly ground black pepper

In a large saucepot over medium heat, heat the oil. Add the shallots and ginger and cook until shallots are soft, 3 to 4 minutes. Stir in the broth and bring to boiling. Stir in the noodles, reduce heat to medium, and simmer, stirring occasionally, until the noodles are cooked, about 2 minutes. Stir in the snow peas, scallions, and chicken. Season with salt and pepper and cook 1 minute longer. Remove the ginger slices and ladle into serving bowls.

Coconut Chicken Soup with Rice Noodles

Serve this Asian-inspired soup, which is loosely based on Thai chicken soups, with hot sauce and lime wedges on the side.

PREP TIME: 10 MINUTES • COOK TIME: 15 MINUTES • MAKES: 4 SERVINGS

2 tablespoons peanut oil

4 shallots, thinly sliced

½ pound boneless, skinless chicken thighs or breasts, cut into 1-inch pieces

4 ounces shiitake mushrooms, stems cut off, tops thinly sliced

Salt

1 can (15 ounces) coconut milk

2 cups chicken broth

4 ounces dried rice noodles (fettuccine size), broken in half

1 can (15 ounces) whole baby corn, drained

½ cup torn basil leaves

2 tablespoons fresh lime juice

1 tablespoon brown sugar

1 tablespoon Thai fish sauce

In a large saucepot over medium-high heat, heat the oil. Add the shallots, chicken, and mushrooms and sprinkle with salt. Cook, stirring, until the shallots are soft, about 4 minutes. Stir in the coconut milk, chicken broth, noodles, and corn and bring to boiling. Reduce heat to medium-low and simmer until the chicken and noodles are cooked through, 6 to 7 minutes. Stir in the basil, lime juice, brown sugar, and fish sauce. Cook 1 minute longer and serve.

Moroccan Lentil Noodle Soup

This soup is best made with fire-roasted tomato sauce.

PREP TIME: 10 MINUTES • COOK TIME: 15 MINUTES • MAKES: 4 TO 6 SERVINGS

2 tablespoons unsalted butter
½ teaspoon ground turmeric
½ teaspoon ground cinnamon
¼ teaspoon saffron, crushed
Pinch red pepper flakes
½ pound boneless, skinless chicken thighs
    (about 3), cut into 1-inch pieces
Salt and freshly ground black pepper
1 large yellow onion, chopped
4 cups chicken broth
1 can (15 ounces) lentils
½ cup fire-roasted tomato sauce
2 ounces capellini or thin spaghetti,
    broken into 2-inch pieces
Lemon wedges, for serving

In a large saucepot over medium-high heat, melt the butter. Stir in the turmeric, cinnamon, saffron, and pepper flakes and cook 30 seconds. Stir in the chicken, sprinkle with salt and pepper, and cook until browned on both sides, 4 to 5 minutes. Stir in the onion and cook until soft, 3 to 4 minutes longer. Stir in the broth, lentils, and tomato sauce and bring to boiling. Add the pasta, reduce heat to medium, and simmer until pasta is al dente, 5 to 7 minutes. Serve with lemon wedges.

Turkey Noodle Soup

Although this soup calls for uncooked cutlets, you can easily make it with leftover cooked turkey instead. Just stir in 2 cups diced cooked turkey along with the peas.

PREP TIME: 5 MINUTES • **COOK TIME: 10 MINUTES** • **MAKES: 8 SERVINGS**

3 tablespoons lemon-flavored avocado
   or olive oil
1 medium yellow onion, chopped
1 pound thinly sliced turkey breast
   cutlets, cut into 1-inch pieces
6 cups chicken broth
Salt and freshly ground black pepper
4 ounces fresh fettuccine, cut in half
2 cups frozen baby peas
¼ cup chopped mint
¼ cup fresh lemon juice or more to taste

In a large saucepot over medium-high heat, heat the lemon oil. Add the onion and cook until soft, 3 to 4 minutes. Stir in the turkey and broth and bring to simmering. Season with salt and pepper, stir in the fettuccine, and cook until al dente, 2 minutes longer. Stir in the peas, mint, and lemon juice. Taste for seasoning and add salt and pepper, if desired. Serve hot.

Southwest Beef and Elbow Soup

If you're lucky enough to have a neighborhood taqueria, bring home a dozen fresh corn tortillas to accompany this soup.

PREP TIME: 5 MINUTES • COOK TIME: 20 MINUTES • MAKES: 8 SERVINGS

2 tablespoons canola oil

1 medium yellow onion, chopped

1 tablespoon minced garlic

½ teaspoon ground cumin

½ teaspoon minced chipotle chile in adobo sauce

1 pound ground beef

Salt and freshly ground black pepper

2 cans (14.5 ounces each) diced fire-roasted tomatoes with chiles

1 can (14.5 ounces) chicken broth

1 can (15 ounces) black beans, rinsed and drained

1 cup elbow macaroni

Sour cream, for serving

Lime wedges, for serving

In a large saucepot over high heat, heat the oil. Add the onion and cook, stirring frequently, until softened, 3 to 4 minutes. Stir in the garlic, cumin, chipotle, and beef. Season with salt and pepper and cook, using a wooden spoon to break up the beef, until beef is browned, about 5 minutes. Stir in the tomatoes, broth, 1 cup water, and black beans and bring to boiling. Add the macaroni, reduce heat to medium, and simmer until almost al dente, about 6 minutes. Turn off the heat and let stand 5 minutes. Serve with sour cream and lime wedges on the side.

Vietnamese Beef Noodle Soup (Faux Pho)

Buy some spring rolls from a Thai restaurant on your way home, then throw together an Asian cabbage salad and this quick soup for a great Asian dinner.

PREP TIME: 5 MINUTES • COOK TIME: 10 MINUTES • MAKES: 4 SERVINGS

4 cups beef broth
2 cups chicken broth
1 star anise
1 cinnamon stick
½ teaspoon ground ginger
4 ounces rice noodles (fettuccine size)
½ pound beef, precut for stir-fry
2 tablespoons fish sauce
Salt and freshly ground pepper
1 cup bean sprouts
1 cup cilantro leaves and stems
1 lime, cut in 4 wedges

In a large saucepot over high heat, combine the beef and chicken broth, star anise, cinnamon, and ginger. Bring to boiling. Stir in the rice noodles and simmer until cooked, 2 minutes. Stir in the beef and fish sauce. Season with salt and pepper and remove from the heat. Ladle into bowls and garnish with the bean sprouts, cilantro, and lime wedges. Serve immediately.

Andouille, Orzo, and Greens Soup

Andouille is a very spicy, Southern-style sausage. For less heat, substitute kielbasa.

PREP TIME: 5 MINUTES • COOK TIME: 20 MINUTES • MAKES: 4 TO 6 SERVINGS

¼ cup extra-virgin olive oil
1 large onion, chopped
2 andouille sausages (about 3 ounces each), diced
½ teaspoon dried thyme
5 cups chicken broth
¼ cup tomato sauce
2 cups frozen chopped mustard greens
½ cup orzo
½ cup frozen petite white corn
Salt and freshly ground black pepper

In a large saucepot over medium-high heat, heat the oil. Add the onion and cook until soft, 3 to 4 minutes. Add the sausages, thyme, broth, tomato sauce, and mustard greens and bring to boiling. Stir in the orzo and cook, stirring occasionally, until al dente, 7 to 9 minutes. Stir in the corn and season with salt and pepper. Turn off heat and let stand 5 minutes before serving.

Sausage, Bean, and Tortellini Soup

This soup is wonderful made with either mild or spicy sausage.

PREP TIME: 10 MINUTES • COOK TIME: 15 MINUTES • MAKES: 6 SERVINGS

2 tablespoons extra-virgin olive oil, plus
   more for drizzling
1 pound mild Italian sausage, sliced into
   ½-inch rounds
1 small red onion, chopped
½ cup red wine
3 cups chicken broth
1 can (28 ounces) diced Italian tomatoes
1 can (15 ounces) white beans, drained
   and rinsed
3 cups (9 ounces) fresh cheese tortellini
2 cups coarsely chopped arugula
Salt and freshly ground black pepper
Grated pecorino Romano cheese, for
   serving

In a large saucepot over medium-high heat, heat the oil. Add the sausage and cook, turning until browned, 6 to 8 minutes. Add the onion to the pan and cook, stirring occasionally, until onion is soft, 2 to 3 minutes. Stir in the wine and simmer until wine is reduced to a glaze, 2 to 3 minutes. Stir in the broth, tomatoes, and beans and bring to boiling. Stir in the tortellini and arugula and cook 2 to 3 minutes longer. Season with salt and pepper and serve with pecorino and olive oil for drizzling on the side.

Alphabet Minestrone

If your supermarket or butcher offers prosciutto ends, buy them for this soup. You'll have the same great flavor from the prosciutto for about half the price.

PREP TIME: 10 MINUTES • COOK TIME: 15 MINUTES • MAKES: 6 TO 8 SERVINGS

¼ cup extra-virgin olive oil, plus more for drizzling
1 large yellow onion, chopped
3 large cloves garlic, minced
½ cup chopped prosciutto
Pinch red pepper flakes
1 can (14.5 ounces) white beans, drained and rinsed
2 cups diced Italian-style tomatoes
4 cups chicken or vegetable broth
½ cup (2 ounces) alphabet pasta
1½ cups frozen cut string beans
1½ cups frozen butternut squash cubes
Salt and freshly ground black pepper
1 cup grated pecorino Romano cheese
¼ cup chopped parsley

1. In a large saucepot over medium-high heat, heat ¼ cup oil. Add the onion, garlic, and prosciutto and cook until the onion is soft, about 5 minutes. Stir in pepper flakes, beans, tomatoes, and chicken broth and bring to boiling.

2. Stir in the pasta, string beans, and squash and simmer until pasta is almost al dente, stirring occasionally, about 5 minutes. Season with salt and pepper and stir in half the pecorino and the parsley. Serve with the remaining pecorino and olive oil for drizzling on the side.

Three-Bean Soup with Tortellini

You can substitute tiny ravioli or short pasta for the tortellini in this very filling bean soup.

PREP TIME: 5 MINUTES • COOK TIME: 25 MINUTES • MAKES: 6 TO 8 SERVINGS

¼ cup extra-virgin olive oil
1 large yellow onion, chopped
1 tablespoon minced garlic
2 carrots, thinly sliced
½ cup chopped Black Forest ham
Pinch red pepper flakes
½ teaspoon ground cumin
1 can (15 ounces) small white beans,
   drained and rinsed
1 can (15 ounces) pinto beans, drained
   and rinsed
1 can (15 ounces) lentils
1 cup tomato sauce
4 cups vegetable or chicken broth
2 cups (8 ounces) dried small (¾-inch)
   cheese tortellini
Salt and freshly ground black pepper
¼ cup chopped Italian parsley
1 cup grated pecorino Romano cheese

1. In a large saucepot over medium-high heat, heat the oil. Add the onion, garlic, carrots, ham, and pepper flakes. Cook until the onion is soft, about 5 minutes. Stir in the cumin, beans, tomato sauce, and broth and bring to boiling.

2. Stir in the tortellini, reduce the heat to medium-low, and simmer until cooked through, about 15 minutes. Season with salt and pepper and stir in the parsley and half the pecorino. Ladle into serving bowls and serve with the remaining pecorino on the side.

Squash, Bean, and Pasta Soup

Make a baby greens salad with a simple vinaigrette and pick up a loaf of artisanal bread to accompany this soup.

PREP TIME: 5 MINUTES • COOK TIME: 20 MINUTES • MAKES: 4 SERVINGS

4 tablespoons extra-virgin olive oil
1 tablespoon minced garlic
1 anchovy fillet
3 pieces (2 x 1 inch each) orange zest
½ teaspoon dried thyme
1 can (15 ounces) chickpeas, rinsed and
   drained
1 package (10 ounces) frozen chopped
   butternut squash
1 cup diced Italian tomatoes
4 cups chicken broth
1 cup (about 4 ounces) tubetti or other
   short pasta
Salt and freshly ground black pepper
¼ cup chopped Italian parsley
1 cup grated pecorino Romano cheese

1. In a large saucepot over medium-high heat, heat 2 tablespoons oil. Stir in the garlic, anchovy fillet, and orange zest and cook 1 minute, mashing the anchovy until dissolved. Stir in the thyme, chickpeas, squash, tomatoes, and broth and bring to boiling. Simmer 10 minutes, stirring and smashing some of the chickpeas against the side of the pot. Stir in the pasta and cook until al dente, 7 to 9 minutes longer.

2. Just before serving, season with salt and pepper and remove the orange zest. Stir in the parsley and half the pecorino. To serve, ladle soup into serving bowls and drizzle with the remaining olive oil, then sprinkle with the remaining pecorino.

Tomato Pasta Soup

This soup is thick and lovely, with big chunks of tomato and small nuggets of pasta. If you prefer a puréed soup, transfer it to a blender or food processor before adding the pasta.

PREP TIME: 5 MINUTES • COOK TIME: 20 MINUTES • MAKES: 4 TO 6 SERVINGS

3 tablespoons extra-virgin olive oil
1 cup chopped yellow onion
Pinch red pepper flakes
1 can (28 ounces) diced peeled tomatoes
1 can (14.5 ounces) chicken broth
Salt
½ cup acini de pepe or other small pasta shape
1 tablespoon chopped tarragon, snipped chives, or chopped Italian parsley (or a mixture of all three)

In a large saucepot over medium-high heat, heat the oil. Add the onion and cook until soft, about 5 minutes. Stir in pepper flakes, tomatoes, chicken broth, and 1 cup of water. Season with salt and bring to a boil. Reduce the heat to medium-low and simmer 5 minutes. Stir in the pasta and simmer until tender, stirring frequently, about 10 minutes longer. Stir in fresh herbs and serve.

VARIATION

Tomato Soup with Pasta and Shrimp
When soup is ready, stir in ¼ pound diced peeled shrimp with the fresh herbs. Turn off the heat and let stand 1 minute or until the shrimp is cooked through.

Pasta e Fagioli

A drizzle of your best extra-virgin olive oil will finish off this classic Italian bean soup.

PREP TIME: 5 MINUTES • COOK TIME: 15 MINUTES • MAKES: 6 SERVINGS

¼ cup extra-virgin olive oil
1 large yellow onion, chopped
3 teaspoons minced garlic
Pinch red pepper flakes
1 can (14.5 ounces) white beans, drained
  and rinsed
1 can (14.5 ounces) chickpeas, drained
  and rinsed
1 can (14.5 ounces) Italian-style diced
  tomatoes
2 cans (14.5 ounces each) chicken broth
Salt
2 cups elbow macaroni
1 cup frozen chopped spinach
1 cup grated Parmesan
  cheese
Freshly ground black
  pepper

1. In a large saucepot over medium-high heat, heat the oil. Add the onion and half the garlic and cook until the onion is soft, about 5 minutes. Stir in the pepper flakes, beans, tomatoes, and chicken broth. Season with salt and bring to boiling.

2. Stir in the pasta. Reduce heat to medium-low and simmer until almost cooked through, 6 to 7 minutes. Stir in the spinach, remaining garlic, and half the Parmesan. Cook 1 minute longer, or until the spinach is heated through. Serve with the remaining Parmesan and black pepper on the side.

Chickpea Soup with Pennette

This thick and nutty Roman-inspired soup needs only good bread and a green salad to complete a meal.

PREP TIME: 5 MINUTES • COOK TIME: 30 MINUTES • MAKES: 4 SERVINGS

2 tablespoons extra-virgin olive oil, plus more for drizzling

1 tablespoon minced garlic

1 anchovy fillet

Pinch red pepper flakes

½ teaspoon dried rosemary

2 cans (15 ounces each) chickpeas, rinsed and drained

4 cups chicken broth

4 ounces pennette

Salt and freshly ground black pepper

Grated pecorino Romano and Parmesan cheese, for serving

In a large saucepot over medium-high heat, heat 2 tablespoons oil. Add the garlic, anchovy fillet, pepper flakes, and rosemary and cook, mashing the anchovy until it dissolves, about 1 minute. Add the chickpeas and cook, stirring, 3 to 4 minutes. Add the broth and 2 cups water and bring to boiling. Reduce the heat to medium-low and simmer 15 minutes, using a wooden spoon to mash some of the chickpeas against the side of the saucepot to thicken the soup. Stir in the pennette and simmer until al dente, about 8 minutes longer. Season with salt and pepper. Ladle into serving bowls and drizzle with olive oil. Serve with pecorino and Parmesan on the side.

Pasta and Potato Chowder

Dollops of pesto are a perfect complement to this creamy chowder.

PREP TIME: 5 MINUTES • COOK TIME: 20 MINUTES • MAKES: 6 SERVINGS

¼ cup extra-virgin olive oil

1 large onion, chopped

½ teaspoon dried oregano

Pinch red pepper flakes

1 can (14½ ounces) chickpeas, drained and rinsed

1 quart chicken broth

1 pound white creamer, Yukon Gold, or Yellow Finn potatoes, washed and cut into ½-inch pieces

1 cup celentani or rotelle

Salt and freshly ground black pepper

½ cup heavy cream

1 jar basil pesto, for serving

In a large saucepot over medium-high heat, heat the olive oil. Add the onion and cook until soft, about 5 minutes. Stir in the oregano, pepper flakes, chickpeas, broth, potatoes, and pasta. Season with salt and pepper and bring to boiling. Reduce the heat to medium-low and simmer until the potatoes and pasta are both tender, about 10 minutes. Stir in the cream and simmer 2 minutes longer. To serve, ladle soup into serving bowls. Serve with the pesto on the side.

Leek, Cabbage, and Pasta Soup

For this soup, chop the leeks and shred the cabbage in the food processor and the prep time will be very short.

PREP TIME: 5 MINUTES • COOK TIME: 15 MINUTES • MAKES: 6 SERVINGS

3 tablespoons unsalted butter

2 medium leeks (white and tender green), rinsed and chopped

½ medium (about 1 pound) Savoy or regular green cabbage, finely shredded

Salt and freshly ground black pepper

1 bay leaf

6 cups chicken broth

Large pinch grated nutmeg

½ cup heavy cream

½ cup acini de pepe or other small pasta shape

2 tablespoons chopped parsley

In a large saucepot over medium-high heat, melt the butter. Add the leeks and cabbage. Season with salt and pepper and cook, stirring frequently, until cabbage is wilted but not browned, 4 to 6 minutes. Stir in the bay leaf, broth, nutmeg, and cream and bring to boiling. Add the pasta and simmer until cooked, 8 to 10 minutes. Stir in the parsley. Remove the bay leaf and serve.

Easy Asian Pasta

Thai Chicken Pesto

Run the bunches of cilantro under cold water to rinse them, then cut the entire top off, stems and all, for the pesto.

PREP TIME: 20 MINUTES • COOK TIME: 8 MINUTES • MAKES: 4 SERVINGS

1 package (7 ounces) rice noodles
   (linguine size)
1 tablespoon minced garlic
2 cups packed cilantro leaves
2 tablespoons pine nuts
1 teaspoon green curry paste
Salt and freshly ground black pepper
¼ cup plus 2 tablespoons peanut or
   canola oil
12 ounces boneless, skinless chicken
   thighs, cut into thin slices
2 cups coarsely chopped washed Asian
   greens or arugula

1. In a large saucepot over high heat, bring 2 quarts of water to boiling. Add the noodles. Let stand 5 minutes, drain, lightly rinse, and transfer to a serving bowl.

2. Meanwhile, in the bowl of a food processor with the steel blade attached, combine the garlic, cilantro, pine nuts, and curry paste. Season with salt and pepper and pulse until finely chopped. With the machine running, pour in ¼ cup oil. Spoon the mixture over the noodles and toss until mixed.

3. In a large skillet over high heat, heat the remaining 2 tablespoons oil until you see a wisp of smoke. Add the chicken. Season with salt and pepper and cook, stirring frequently, until browned and cooked through, 3 to 4 minutes. Add the chicken and the salad greens to the noodle mixture, toss until combined, and serve.

Turkey with Chili Noodles

This spicy dish is a great way to serve boneless turkey breasts.

PREP TIME: 5 MINUTES • COOK TIME: 15 MINUTES • MAKES: 4 SERVINGS

Salt
½ pound spaghetti
2 tablespoons peanut or canola oil
8 ounces boneless, skinless turkey breast,
    cut into thin bite-sized pieces
2 cups diced frozen sweet potatoes
4 teaspoons jarred roasted red chili paste
2 tablespoons fish sauce
½ teaspoon sugar
1 can (13. 5 ounces) canned coconut milk,
    well shaken
½ cup thinly sliced scallions
Lime wedges, for serving

1. In a large saucepot over high heat, bring 2 quarts of water to boiling. Add salt to taste and the pasta. Cook until al dente, 7 to 9 minutes, and drain.

2. In a large nonstick skillet or wok over high heat, heat the oil. Add the turkey, sprinkle with salt, and cook until no longer pink, about 2 minutes. Transfer to a bowl. In the same skillet over medium heat, combine the sweet potatoes, chili paste, fish sauce, sugar, and coconut milk. Bring to simmering and simmer until the sweet potatoes are cooked through, 4 to 5 minutes. Stir in the spaghetti, turkey, and scallions and simmer 1 minute longer. Spoon onto a serving platter and serve hot with lime wedges.

VARIATION

Chicken with Chili Noodles
Substitute 8 ounces boneless, skinless chicken breasts for the turkey. Prepare as directed above.

Soba Noodles with Sausage and Broccoli Raab

Broccoli raab has a slightly bitter flavor that's great combined with ginger and soba noodles. Substitute broccoli florets if broccoli raab is unavailable.

PREP TIME: 5 MINUTES • COOK TIME: 20 MINUTES • MAKES: 2 TO 3 SERVINGS

Salt

8 ounces soba noodles

2 tablespoons olive oil

2 spicy or mild Italian sausages, cut in half lengthwise, then in ½-inch pieces

1 tablespoon minced garlic

1 tablespoon minced fresh ginger

1 bunch broccoli raab, cut into 1-inch pieces

2 tablespoons sherry

¾ cup chicken broth

1. In a large saucepot over high heat, bring 2 quarts of water to boiling. Add salt to taste and the soba noodles. Cook until the noodles are just cooked through, 2 to 3 minutes. Drain, rinse with cold water, and set aside.

2. Meanwhile, in a large skillet over medium-high heat, heat the oil. Add the sausages and cook until browned, about 5 to 6 minutes. Stir in the garlic and ginger and cook 1 minute. Add the broccoli raab, sherry, and broth. Cover and simmer, stirring occasionally, until the stalks are tender, about 5 to 8 minutes. Stir in the noodles to reheat and adjust the seasoning for salt. Divide among serving dishes and serve immediately.

VARIATION

Soba Noodles with Broccoli Raab and Walnuts
In a small dry skillet over medium-high heat, toast 2 tablespoons chopped walnuts until lightly browned, about 5 minutes. Transfer to a bowl. Continue as directed above. Just before serving, sprinkle walnuts over the noodles.

Noodles with Peppers and Barbecued Pork

Packaged steamed stir-fry noodles are usually found in the refrigerated section.

PREP TIME: 15 MINUTES • COOK TIME: 5 MINUTES • MAKES: 2 TO 3 SERVINGS

½ cup chicken broth

4 tablespoons spicy oyster sauce

2 teaspoons sesame oil

1 tablespoon cornstarch

2 tablespoons peanut or canola oil

2 tablespoons minced garlic

1 tablespoon minced fresh ginger

2 cups frozen pepper strips

8 ounces steamed fresh Chinese noodles
   or cooked spaghetti

½ cup shredded Chinese barbecued pork

2 scallions, thinly sliced crosswise

1. In a small bowl, stir together the broth, oyster sauce, sesame oil, and cornstarch. Set aside.

2. In a large skillet over high heat, heat the peanut oil until you see a wisp of smoke. Add the garlic and ginger and cook until the garlic is golden, about 30 seconds. Stir in pepper strips, noodles, pork, and sauce and bring to simmering. Simmer 2 to 3 minutes and stir in the scallions. Spoon onto a serving platter and serve.

Spaghetti with Pork, Black Beans, and Broccolini

Broccolini, also called asparation and baby broccoli, is a combination of broccoli and Chinese kale and has tender stalks and a mild broccoli flavor.

PREP TIME: 5 MINUTES • COOK TIME: 15 MINUTES • MAKES: 4 SERVINGS

Salt
½ pound spaghetti
2 tablespoons peanut or canola oil
1 tablespoon minced garlic
¼ teaspoon red pepper flakes
1 pound ground pork
½ pound broccolini, cut into 1-inch pieces
½ cup chicken broth
¼ cup Chinese black bean sauce
1 teaspoon sugar
2 scallions, thinly sliced
1 tablespoon red wine vinegar

1. In a large saucepot over high heat, bring 2 quarts of water to boiling. Add salt to taste and the spaghetti. Cook until al dente, 6 to 9 minutes. Drain and transfer to a large platter.

2. In a large skillet or wok over high heat, heat the oil until you see a wisp of smoke. Add the garlic, pepper flakes, and pork. Stir-fry until pork is no longer pink, breaking up the mixture as it cooks, about 3 to 4 minutes. Transfer to a plate and add the broccolini and the broth to the skillet. Simmer until broccolini is crisp-tender, 4 to 5 minutes. Return the pork to the skillet, stir in the black bean sauce, sugar, and scallions and simmer 1 minute. Stir in the vinegar and toss. Spoon mixture over the spaghetti and serve immediately.

Beef and Shiitake Noodles

Beef and shiitakes are a great combination. If you can't find fresh shiitakes, substitute dried shiitakes and soak them in hot water before slicing.

PREP TIME: 10 MINUTES • COOK TIME: 6 MINUTES • MAKES: 4 SERVINGS

Salt
8 ounces soba noodles
Freshly ground black pepper
½ pound beef, precut for stir-fry
3 tablespoons teriyaki sauce
1 tablespoon minced ginger
2 teaspoons sesame oil
3 tablespoons peanut or canola oil
1 tablespoon minced garlic
6 shiitake (about 6 medium) mushrooms, stems discarded and thinly sliced
3 scallions, cut in 2-inch lengths
⅓ cup chicken broth

1. In a large saucepot over high heat, bring 2 quarts of water to boiling. Add salt to taste and the noodles. Cook until tender, 2 to 3 minutes. Drain, rinse with cold water, and set aside.

2. In a small bowl, toss together the beef and 1 tablespoon teriyaki sauce. In another small bowl, combine the ginger, remaining teriyaki sauce, and sesame oil.

3. In a wok or large nonstick skillet over high heat, heat 1 tablespoon peanut oil. Sprinkle the beef with salt and pepper and cook until browned, 1 to 2 minutes. Remove to a plate and add the remaining 2 tablespoons peanut oil to the wok. Add the garlic, mushrooms, and scallions and cook, stirring constantly, 2 to 3 minutes, or until the vegetables are crisp-tender. Stir in the ginger mixture, beef, chicken broth, and noodles and stir 1 minute longer. Serve hot.

Wasabi Steaks with Noodles

This is a perfect dish for entertaining. You can grill or panfry the steaks instead of broiling.

PREP TIME: 15 MINUTES • COOK TIME: 10 MINUTES • MAKES: 4 SERVINGS

2 tablespoons unsalted butter, softened
½ teaspoon prepared wasabi
1 package rice noodles (fettuccine size)
2 tablespoons thinly sliced pickled
   ginger, plus 2 tablespoons ginger juice
2 tablespoons soy sauce
1 tablespoon rice vinegar
1 tablespoon canola oil
1 teaspoon minced fresh ginger
½ English cucumber, peeled
Freshly ground black pepper
4 boneless top sirloin steaks (1 inch
   thick, about 1½ pounds)
Salt

1. Heat the broiler. Line a broiler pan with foil.

2. In a small bowl, mix together the butter and wasabi. Spoon the mixture onto wax paper and roll it into a short log. Twist the ends and place in the freezer.

3. In a large saucepot over high heat, bring 2 quarts of water to boiling. Add the noodles and remove from the heat. Let soak for 5 minutes. Drain and rinse with cold water. Let drain and transfer to a large bowl. Add the pickled ginger and juice, soy sauce, vinegar, oil, and fresh ginger. Using a vegetable peeler, slice the cucumber lengthwise into ribbons until you get to the seed core. Discard the core and mix the ribbons into the noodle mixture. Season with pepper.

4. Sprinkle the steaks with salt and pepper and place on prepared broiler pan. Broil 1 to 2 inches from the heat until browned, turning once, 6 to 8 minutes total for medium-rare.

5. To serve, divide the noodle mixture among plates and place a steak on top. Cut the wasabi butter into 4 pieces and place a slice on each steak. Serve immediately.

Chow Mein with Crisp Noodle Cake

For a just-as-tasty vegetarian version, use vegetable broth and leave out the shrimp and pork.

PREP TIME: 10 MINUTES • COOK TIME: 20 MINUTES • MAKES: 4 SERVINGS

⅓ cup chicken broth
2 tablespoons soy sauce
1 teaspoon sugar
1 teaspoon cornstarch
Freshly ground black pepper
½ cup peanut or canola oil
4 cups cooked spaghetti
1 small red onion, cut in half lengthwise
   and thinly sliced
1 stalk celery, thinly sliced on the diagonal
1 cup (about 2 ounces) snow peas
½ pound shelled and deveined medium
   shrimp
½ cup thinly sliced Chinese barbecued pork
1 cup bean sprouts

1. In a small bowl, whisk together the broth, soy sauce, sugar, and cornstarch. Season with pepper and set aside.

2. In a large skillet over high heat, heat the oil. Add the pasta and, using a spatula, press down to form a flat cake. Cook until browned on the bottom, 6 to 7 minutes. Using two spatulas, carefully turn cake over and brown on the other side, another 6 to 7 minutes. Transfer to a serving platter, cover with foil, and keep warm. Pour off all but about 2 tablespoons of the oil.

3. In the same skillet over high heat, combine the onion, celery, and snow peas and toss 1 minute. Stir in the shrimp and pork. Cook until the shrimp are pink, 1 to 2 minutes longer. Stir in the broth mixture and bring to simmering. Simmer 1 minute and stir in the bean sprouts. Spoon the shrimp mixture over the noodle cake. Serve immediately.

Shrimp Pad Thai

Chopped toasted peanuts, sliced scallions, or shredded carrots are all good additional garnishes.

PREP TIME: 5 MINUTES • COOK TIME: 15 MINUTES • MAKES: 4 SERVINGS

½ pound rice noodles (fettuccine size)
3 tablespoons fish sauce
3 tablespoons ketchup
2 tablespoons light brown sugar
2 tablespoons canola or peanut oil
1 tablespoon chopped garlic
12 large shelled and deveined shrimp
1 large egg, lightly beaten
1 lime, cut into wedges, for garnish
1 package (12 ounces) bean sprouts
1 cup cilantro leaves, for garnish

1. In a large saucepot over high heat, bring 2 quarts of water to boiling. Add the noodles and remove from the heat. Let the noodles soak for 5 minutes. Drain and rinse with cold water. Drain again.

2. In a small bowl, combine the fish sauce, ketchup, sugar, and 2 tablespoons water.

3. Heat a wok or large nonstick skillet over high heat. Add 1 tablespoon oil and the garlic. Cook until garlic is golden, 30 seconds. Add the shrimp and toss until opaque, 1 to 2 minutes. Push the shrimp to the side of the pan and add the egg. Cook the egg, stirring, until firm. Mix it with the shrimp and transfer the mixture to a plate.

4. Add the remaining oil to the pan and heat until you see a wisp of smoke. Add the noodles. Using tongs, toss the noodles until they soften. Add the ketchup mixture and toss until coated. Return the shrimp mixture to the pan and toss until heated through, about 1 minute. Squeeze 1 lime wedge over and transfer to a platter. Sprinkle with the sprouts and cilantro and serve with lime wedges.

VARIATION

Chicken Pad Thai
Substitute 1½ cups diced cooked chicken for the shrimp. Add it when you add the cooked egg to the noodles.

Fried Rice Noodles with Sugar Snaps and Shrimp

Fried rice noodles are like a variation on fried rice—kids love it.

PREP TIME: 10 MINUTES • COOK TIME: 10 MINUTES • MAKES: 2 TO 3 SERVINGS

4 ounces rice noodles (vermicelli size)
2 tablespoons peanut or canola oil
2 tablespoons minced garlic
12 ounces shelled small shrimp
1 bag (8 ounces) frozen sugar snap peas
　　(about 2 cups)
½ cup chicken broth
2 tablespoons soy sauce
½ teaspoon sugar
½ teaspoon coarse salt
½ teaspoon freshly ground black pepper
½ cup sliced scallions (3 to 4 whole)
1 teaspoon sesame oil

1. In a large saucepot over high heat, bring 2 quarts of water to boiling. Add the rice noodles. Remove from the heat, let stand 8 minutes, drain, and rinse with cold water.

2. Heat a large nonstick skillet or wok over high heat. Add 1 tablespoon of the oil and heat 15 seconds. Add the garlic and shrimp and cook until the shrimp are pink, about 1½ minutes. Using a slotted spoon, transfer shrimp to a bowl.

3. Add the remaining tablespoon of oil and heat until you see a wisp of smoke. Stir in the peas, broth, soy sauce, and sugar. Season with salt and pepper. Cook, stirring frequently, until the peas are tender, 4 to 5 minutes. Stir in the scallions, sesame oil, noodles, and shrimp and toss until the noodles have absorbed the sauce, about 1 minute longer.

Vietnamese-Style Scallops with Somen Noodles

Serve this mild dish with sriracha (a hot pepper sauce found in the international aisle or Asian supermarkets) on the side so diners can adjust the heat to their own tastes.

PREP TIME: 15 MINUTES • COOK TIME: 10 MINUTES • MAKES: 4 SERVINGS

Salt
8 ounces (2 bundles) somen noodles
2 tablespoons peanut or canola oil
1 cup thinly sliced shallots
2 tablespoons minced garlic
¾ pound sea scallops, cut in half horizontally
¾ cup chicken broth
2 tablespoons fish sauce
2 scallions, thinly sliced crosswise
Freshly ground black pepper
½ cup cilantro leaves
¼ cup mint leaves
Lime wedges and sriracha, for serving

1. In a large saucepot over high heat, bring 2 quarts of water to boiling. Add salt to taste and the noodles. Cook 1 to 2 minutes. Drain and set aside.

2. In a large skillet or wok over high heat, heat the oil. Add the shallots and garlic and cook until garlic is golden, about 2 minutes. Add the scallops and cook 1 minute. Stir in the broth, fish sauce, and scallions. Season with pepper and bring to simmering. Stir in the noodles and simmer 1 minute longer. Sprinkle with cilantro and mint and toss. Spoon onto a serving platter and serve with lime wedges and sriracha on the side.

Noodles with Mushrooms and Greens

You can substitute 8 ounces fresh fettuccine or tagliatelle for the lasagna noodles. Just remember that the cooking time will be shorter.

PREP TIME: 5 MINUTES • COOK TIME: 15 MINUTES • MAKES: 2 TO 3 SERVINGS

Salt
8 traditional curly-edged lasagna noodles (about 9 ounces), broken into rough 4-inch pieces
3 tablespoons peanut or canola oil
1 package (8 ounces) sliced portobellos
1 tablespoon minced garlic
1 tablespoon minced fresh ginger
Freshly ground black pepper
1 cup (packed) washed Asian salad greens or arugula
3 tablespoons shiitake-sesame vinaigrette

1. In a large saucepot over high heat, bring 2 quarts of water to boiling. Add salt to taste and the noodles and cook until al dente, 9 to 10 minutes. Drain well.

2. Meanwhile, in a large skillet over medium-high heat, heat the oil. Add the mushrooms and cook on one side until browned and soft, about 3 minutes. Turn mushrooms over and brown on the other side, 2 to 3 minutes longer. Stir in the garlic and ginger. Season with salt and pepper. Spoon into a large serving dish and add the greens.

3. Pour the drained pasta over the greens and mushrooms. Add the vinaigrette. Season with salt and pepper and toss until mixed. Serve immediately.

Curry Noodles with Bok Choy and Tofu

Chopped cilantro is a perfect garnish for this (mostly) vegetarian dish.

PREP TIME: 10 MINUTES • COOK TIME: 15 MINUTES • MAKES: 4 SERVINGS

1 cup chicken broth

2 tablespoons soy sauce

1 teaspoon sugar

1 teaspoon cornstarch

Freshly ground black pepper

Salt

8 ounces flat Chinese egg noodles or
    fettuccine

2 tablespoons peanut or canola oil

1 small yellow onion, cut in half lengthwise
    and thinly sliced

2 tablespoons curry powder

1 tablespoon minced garlic

1 tablespoon finely chopped fresh ginger

4 baby bok choy, cut into 1-inch pieces

1 package (7 ounces) teriyaki-flavored
    baked tofu, cut into 1/2-inch cubes

1. In a small bowl, whisk together the broth, soy sauce, sugar, and cornstarch. Season with pepper and set aside.

2. In a large saucepot over high heat, bring 2 quarts of water to boiling. Add salt to taste and the noodles. Cook until al dente, 6 to 9 minutes. Drain and set aside.

3. In a large skillet or wok over high heat, heat the oil until you see a wisp of smoke. Add the onion and cook until soft and starting to brown, about 2 minutes. Add the curry powder, garlic, and ginger and cook 30 seconds. Stir in the bok choy and tofu and cook 2 minutes, stirring constantly. Stir in the broth mixture and bring to boiling, stirring frequently. Simmer until the bok choy is crisp-tender, about 2 minutes longer. Add the noodles and toss 1 minute. Spoon into a serving dish and serve immediately.

Elegant Pasta

Cavatelli with Cauliflower and Fried Capers

Basil-flavored olive oil adds a lovely subtle basil flavor to this dish.

PREP TIME: 10 MINUTES • COOK TIME: 15 MINUTES • MAKES: 4 SERVINGS

Salt

1 pound cavatelli

6 tablespoons basil-flavored extra-virgin olive oil

1/4 cup capers, drained on paper towels

1 tablespoon minced garlic

Pinch red pepper flakes

1 package (16 ounces) frozen chopped cauliflower

1/2 cup white wine

1/2 cup chopped pitted green olives

2 tablespoons heavy cream

Freshly ground black pepper

1/2 cup grated Parmesan cheese, plus more for serving

24 basil leaves, torn, for garnish

1. In a large saucepot over high heat, bring 4 quarts water to boiling. Add salt to taste and the cavatelli. Cook until al dente, 6 to 8 minutes. Drain well and transfer to a large serving bowl.

2. Meanwhile, in a large skillet over medium-high heat, heat the oil until very hot but not smoking. Add the capers and cook until they turn gray, 2 to 3 minutes. Using a slotted spoon, remove capers to a paper towel–lined plate. Add the garlic and pepper flakes to the skillet and cook 30 seconds. Stir in the cauliflower, white wine, olives, and heavy cream. Cover and simmer until the cauliflower is cooked through, 6 to 8 minutes. Season with salt and pepper. Pour the sauce over the cavatelli, add 1/2 cup Parmesan and the basil, and toss until mixed. Sprinkle with capers and serve with additional Parmesan on the side.

Pasta Bolognese

Traditional Bolognese sauces cook for 1½ to 2 hours. This one is considerably faster.

PREP TIME: 5 MINUTES • COOK TIME: 40 MINUTES • MAKES: 8 SERVINGS

1 large carrot, cut in 2-inch pieces
1 large rib celery, cut in 2-inch pieces
½ yellow onion, peeled and cut in half
3 tablespoons extra-virgin olive oil
2 ounces pancetta, coarsely chopped
½ pound chicken livers
½ pound ground chuck
½ pound ground pork
Salt and freshly ground black pepper
½ cup dry white wine
½ cup milk
1 jar (25 ounces) tomato pasta sauce
2 pounds fresh tagliatelle or fettuccine

1. In the bowl of a food processor with the steel blade attached, combine the carrot, celery, and onion. Process until finely chopped. In a large skillet over medium-high heat, heat the oil. Add the pancetta and cook until it has softened, about 3 minutes. Add the vegetables and cook until the onion is soft, stirring frequently, about 3 minutes.

2. Meanwhile, pour the chicken livers into the bowl of the processor and pulse until coarsely chopped. Add to the skillet along with the beef and pork. Cook, stirring, until the meat is no longer pink, about 6 minutes. Season with salt and pepper. Add the wine and simmer until the liquid is reduced by half, about 3 minutes. Add the milk and simmer until the liquid has reduced by half again, about 3 minutes more. Add the tomato sauce. Pour ½ cup water into the tomato sauce jar, swish it around, and add the water to the skillet. Simmer until sauce is thick, about 15 minutes. Season with salt and pepper.

3. Meanwhile, in a large saucepot over high heat, bring 5 quarts water to boiling. Add salt to taste and the pasta. Cook until al dente, 5 to 6 minutes. Drain well and transfer to a serving bowl. Spoon the sauce over the pasta, toss until mixed, and serve.

Pasta with Cauliflower, Salami, Peas, and Basil

For a vegetarian version, omit the salami and use vegetable broth instead of the chicken broth.

PREP TIME: 10 MINUTES • COOK TIME: 12 MINUTES • MAKES: 4 SERVINGS

Salt
1 pound orecchiette or cavatelli
2 tablespoons unsalted butter
3 tablespoons olive oil
1 tablespoon minced garlic
Pinch red pepper flakes
¾ cup diced salami
5 cups (about 1 pound) cauliflower florets
½ cup white wine
½ cup chicken broth
¼ cup heavy cream
1 cup frozen baby peas
Freshly ground black pepper
1 cup grated Parmesan cheese
16 basil leaves, torn

1. In a large saucepot over high heat, bring 4 quarts water to boiling. Add salt to taste and the pasta. Cook until al dente, 6 to 9 minutes. Drain and return to the saucepot.

2. Meanwhile, in a large skillet, over medium-high heat, heat the butter and olive oil. Add the garlic, pepper flakes, and salami. Cook 1 minute. Add cauliflower, toss to mix, and pour in the wine. Simmer until the liquid is reduced by half, about 3 minutes. Add the chicken broth and cream and simmer until the cauliflower is tender but not mushy, 3 to 5 minutes. Stir in the peas, season with salt and pepper, and cook 1 minute longer. Pour the cauliflower mixture over the pasta. Add the Parmesan and basil and toss until mixed. Serve immediately.

Pink Angel-Hair

If you add ham to this dish, make sure to dice it very small.

PREP TIME: 5 MINUTES • COOK TIME: 10 MINUTES • MAKES: 4 SERVINGS

Salt
1 pound capellini
¼ cup extra-virgin olive oil
1 tablespoon minced garlic
Pinch red pepper flakes
1 teaspoon sugar
1 can (28 ounces) diced Italian tomatoes
Freshly ground black pepper
½ cup mascarpone cheese
½ cup grated Parmesan cheese, plus more
   for serving

1. In a large saucepot over high heat, bring 4 quarts of water to boiling. Add salt to taste and the capellini. Cook until al dente, about 4 to 5 minutes. Drain and transfer to a large serving bowl.

2. Meanwhile, in a large skillet over medium-high heat, heat the oil. Add the garlic and pepper flakes and cook 30 seconds. Stir in the sugar and tomatoes. Season with salt and pepper and simmer 5 minutes. Stir in the mascarpone. Pour the sauce over the capellini, add ½ cup Parmesan, and toss until mixed. Serve immediately with additional Parmesan on the side.

VARIATION

Pink Angel-Hair with Ham
Add ¾ cup diced Black Forest ham to the sauce along with the mascarpone.

Capellini with Saffron and Crab

This is great for a light lunch or brunch. You can use fresh capellini in place of the dried—just remember the cooking time will be slightly shorter.

PREP TIME: 10 MINUTES • COOK TIME: 10 MINUTES • MAKES: 4 SERVINGS

½ stick (¼ cup) unsalted butter
½ cup finely chopped shallots
1 cup canned diced tomatoes
½ cup heavy cream
⅛ teaspoon saffron threads
1 can (6 ounces) crabmeat, drained, liquid
    reserved
Salt and freshly ground black pepper
8 ounces capellini
2 tablespoons chopped Italian parsley
Grated Parmesan cheese,
    for serving

1. In a medium skillet over medium-high heat, melt the butter. Cook the shallots until soft, 3 to 4 minutes. Stir in the tomatoes, cream, saffron, and reserved crab liquid and bring to simmering. Simmer until liquid is slightly reduced, about 3 minutes. Stir in the crab and season with salt and pepper.

2. Meanwhile, in a large saucepot over high heat, bring 2 quarts water to boiling. Add salt to taste and the capellini. Cook until al dente, 2 to 3 minutes. Drain well and transfer to a large serving dish. Spoon sauce over the capellini. Sprinkle with parsley and toss until mixed. Serve with Parmesan on the side.

Spaghettini with Spicy Squid Sauce

Try to buy small squid for the best flavor and don't cook them longer than two minutes or they'll become very rubbery.

PREP TIME: 5 MINUTES • COOK TIME: 20 MINUTES • MAKES: 4 SERVINGS

Salt
1 pound spaghettini
3 tablespoons extra-virgin olive oil
6 cloves garlic, peeled and crushed lightly
½ teaspoon red pepper flakes
1 can (28 ounces) diced tomatoes
1 teaspoon sugar
Freshly ground black pepper
½ pound squid, cleaned and cut into rings
16 fresh basil leaves, for garnish

1. In a large saucepot over high heat, bring 4 quarts water to boiling. Add salt to taste and the spaghettini. Cook until al dente, 7 to 9 minutes. Drain well and transfer to serving dishes.

2. Meanwhile, in a large skillet over medium-high heat, heat the oil. Add the garlic and cook until golden, about 2 minutes. Stir in the pepper flakes, tomatoes, and sugar. Season with salt and pepper and cook until the liquid is slightly reduced, 9 to 10 minutes. Stir in the squid and cook until the squid is opaque, 2 minutes longer. Remove the garlic cloves, if desired.

3. Spoon sauce over each serving and top each with 4 basil leaves. Toss lightly and serve immediately.

East Indian Chicken Curry Noodles

If you use hot Madras curry powder, this dish will be both very flavorful and very fiery.

PREP TIME: 5 MINUTES • COOKING TIME: 20 MINUTES • MAKES: 4 SERVINGS

Salt
12 ounces egg noodles or fettuccine
½ stick (¼ cup) unsalted butter
1 large yellow onion, cut in half and thinly
   sliced
2 tablespoons curry powder
1 cup chicken broth
1 cup canned diced tomatoes
Freshly ground black pepper
2 cups diced cooked chicken
¼ cup crème fraîche or sour cream
½ cup cilantro leaves, for garnish

1. In a large saucepot over high heat, bring 3 quarts water to boiling. Add salt to taste and the noodles. Cook until al dente, 6 to 9 minutes. Drain and return to the saucepot.

2. Meanwhile, in a large skillet over medium-high heat, melt the butter. Add the onion and cook until soft, 4 to 5 minutes. Stir in the curry powder and cook 1 minute. Stir in the broth and tomatoes and season with salt and pepper. Simmer until lightly thickened, about 5 minutes. Stir in the chicken and crème fraîche and cook 1 minute longer. Pour the curry mixture over the noodles and toss until mixed. Transfer to a serving bowl, sprinkle with cilantro leaves, and serve immediately.

Moroccan Beef with Couscous

If you're using fine salt, reduce the amount for the couscous to ¼ teaspoon and for the spice rub to ½ teaspoon. Harissa, a hot pepper paste, can be found in the international foods section of the supermarket.

PREP TIME: 5 MINUTES • COOK TIME: 15 MINUTES • MAKES: 4 SERVINGS

1 cup instant couscous
2 tablespoons unsalted butter
⅓ cup sliced almonds
Pinch red pepper flakes
Grated zest of 1 orange
1½ cups chicken broth
Coarse salt and freshly ground black pepper
1 teaspoon ground coriander
½ teaspoon ground cumin
4 boneless top sirloin steaks
   (1 inch thick, about 1½ pounds)
Harissa, for serving

1. Place the couscous in a medium heat-proof bowl. In a large skillet over medium-high heat, melt 1 tablespoon butter. Add the almonds and cook until the almonds are lightly browned, about 2 minutes. Stir in the pepper flakes, zest, and broth and bring to boiling. Season with ½ teaspoon each salt and pepper and pour over the couscous. Cover the bowl and let stand until the broth is absorbed, 3 to 5 minutes. Fluff couscous with a fork and cover bowl to keep it warm.

2. In a small bowl, stir together 1 teaspoon coarse salt, ½ teaspoon black pepper, the coriander, and cumin. Rub both sides of each steak with the mixture.

3. Wipe out the skillet and, over high heat, melt the remaining butter. When the butter stops bubbling, add the steaks and cook, turning once, 8 to 9 minutes total for medium-rare. To serve, divide the couscous among four plates, and top each serving with a steak. Serve with harissa on the side.

Scallop Couscous

Serve this cross-cultural dish with a green salad or grilled asparagus. If your supermarket only has frozen scallops, defrost them in a bowl of cold water for 10 to 15 minutes, then cut them in half crosswise.

PREP TIME: 5 MINUTES • COOK TIME: 10 MINUTES • MAKES: 4 SERVINGS

1 cup couscous
4 tablespoons unsalted butter
1 tablespoon finely chopped fresh ginger
⅓ cup pine nuts
Pinch red pepper flakes
1 cup frozen baby peas
1½ cups chicken broth
Salt and freshly ground black pepper
1 pound large sea scallops, cut in half
   crosswise
1 tablespoon chopped fresh parsley
1 to 2 tablespoons lemon juice

1. Place the couscous in a heatproof serving bowl. Melt 1 tablespoon of the butter in a large skillet over medium-high heat. Add the ginger, pine nuts, and pepper flakes and cook until the ginger and pine nuts are lightly browned, about 2 minutes. Stir in the peas and broth and bring to boiling. Season with salt and pepper and pour over the couscous. Cover with foil and let stand until the broth is absorbed, 3 to 5 minutes. Fluff with a fork and keep warm.

2. Meanwhile, in the same skillet over high heat, melt the remaining butter. Pat the scallops dry and sprinkle with salt and pepper. Arrange the scallops in one layer in the skillet and cook 1 minute without moving them. Using tongs, turn over and sear the other side. Cook until opaque, 1 minute longer. Transfer to a plate and cover with foil. Stir the parsley, lemon juice, and any juices that have collected on the plate of scallops into the skillet and stir. Divide the couscous among serving plates. Place scallops on top and pour the sauce over. Serve immediately.

Penne with Black Pepper and Walnuts

A crunchy iceberg lettuce salad pairs nicely with this peppery pasta.

PREP TIME: 5 MINUTES • COOKING TIME: 12 MINUTES • MAKES: 4 SERVINGS

½ cup coarsely chopped walnuts
Salt
12 ounces penne
1 package (5.2 ounces) black
   pepper-flavored soft cheese
2 tablespoons heavy cream
2 tablespoons finely chopped Italian
   parsley, for garnish

1. In a small skillet over medium-high heat, toast the walnuts until lightly browned, about 5 minutes. Transfer to a bowl.

2. In a large saucepot over high heat, bring 2 quarts water to boiling. Add salt to taste and the penne and cook until al dente, 6 to 8 minutes. Drain.

3. Meanwhile, in a large serving bowl, stir together the cheese, cream, and salt. Pour penne over the cheese mixture and toss until mixed. Sprinkle with the walnuts and parsley and serve immediately.

Penne with Herbed Garlic Cheese

Soft herb cheese makes this penne very flavorful and very fast.

PREP TIME: 5 MINUTES • **COOK TIME: 9 MINUTES** • **MAKES: 4 SERVINGS**

Salt
12 ounces penne
1 package (5.2 ounces) herb and garlic
  cheese
2 tablespoons heavy cream
½ cup chopped pitted green olives
Freshly ground black pepper
2 tablespoons finely chopped Italian
  parsley, for garnish

1. In a large saucepot over high heat, bring 3 quarts water to boiling. Add salt to taste and the penne and cook until al dente, 6 to 8 minutes. Drain.

2. Meanwhile, in a large serving bowl, stir together the herb cheese, cream, and olives. Season with salt and pepper. Add the penne and toss until mixed. Sprinkle with the parsley and serve.

Spaghetti with Pancetta and Arugula Pesto

Arugula pesto is bright green and lightly zingy depending on how sharp the arugula is.

PREP TIME: 15 MINUTES • COOK TIME: 15 MINUTES • MAKES: 4 SERVINGS

2 tablespoons pine nuts
2 cups (packed) washed arugula
2 cloves garlic, peeled
¼ cup heavy cream
3 tablespoons unsalted butter, softened
Salt and freshly ground black pepper
1 pound spaghetti
4 ounces pancetta or 4 thick slices bacon,
  coarsely chopped

1. In the bowl of a food processor with the steel blade attached, combine the pine nuts, arugula, and garlic and process until finely chopped. With the motor running, add the cream, pouring in a steady stream. Add 2 tablespoons butter and a large pinch each of salt and pepper and pulse until combined.

2. In a large saucepot over high heat, bring 2 quarts water to boiling. Add salt to taste and the spaghetti. Cook until al dente, 6 to 9 minutes. Drain well and transfer to a large serving bowl.

3. Meanwhile, in a medium skillet over high heat, heat the remaining tablespoon butter. Add the pancetta and cook until crisp, about 5 minutes. Transfer to a paper towel-lined plate.

4. Spoon the pesto over the spaghetti and toss until mixed. Sprinkle with the pancetta and serve.

VARIATION

Spaghetti with Pancetta, Arugula Pesto, and Baby Peas
Prepare pesto as above. When the spaghetti is al dente, add ¾ cup frozen baby peas to the cooking water and then drain with the spaghetti. Continue as directed above.

Parslied Spaghetti with Roasted Salmon

If you feel like splurging a little, buy line-caught wild salmon, preferably King or Sockeye fillet. To make sure to have equal portions, cut the whole piece in half and then cut each of the halves in half.

PREP TIME: 5 MINUTES • COOKING TIME: 20 MINUTES • MAKES: 4 SERVINGS

⅓ cup garlic-flavored olive oil or extra-virgin olive oil
½ teaspoon red pepper flakes
1½ pounds skin-on salmon fillet
Salt and freshly ground black pepper
1 pound spaghetti
¼ cup finely chopped Italian parsley
Grated Parmesan cheese, for serving

1. Heat the oven to 500°F. In a large nonstick ovenproof skillet over medium heat, heat the oil and pepper flakes until the oil sizzles, about 2 minutes. Carefully pour the oil into a glass measuring cup.

2. Sprinkle the salmon with salt and pepper. Return 1½ tablespoons oil to the skillet and heat over high. Add the salmon flesh-side down and put the skillet into the oven. Cook 5 minutes, turn, and roast until the salmon is cooked through, 3 to 6 minutes longer. Transfer to a cutting board.

3. Meanwhile, in a large saucepot over high heat, bring 4 quarts water to boiling. Add salt to taste and the spaghetti. Cook until al dente, 6 to 9 minutes. Drain and return to the saucepot. Pour the remaining oil over the spaghetti, add the parsley, season with salt and pepper, and toss. Divide among serving dishes. Cut the salmon into 4 portions and place a piece on top of each serving. Serve with Parmesan on the side.

Spaghetti with Lobster Sauce

To thaw lobster tails, put them in a bowl of cold water for 30 minutes or thaw overnight in the fridge. Use kitchen scissors to cut the tails open, cutting straight up the middle of each shell. Remove the meat and then use the scissors to cut the shells into 2-inch pieces.

PREP TIME: 10 MINUTES • COOK TIME: 20 MINUTES • MAKES: 4 SERVINGS

3 tablespoons extra-virgin olive oil
2 frozen rock lobster tails (see above)
4 cloves garlic, peeled and lightly crushed
Pinch red pepper flakes
1 can (28 ounces) diced tomatoes
1 teaspoon sugar
Salt and freshly ground black pepper
1 pound spaghetti
1 tablespoon chopped fresh basil

1. In a large skillet over medium-high heat, heat the oil. Add the lobster shells, garlic, and pepper flakes. Cook until the garlic is golden, 2 minutes. Stir in the tomatoes and sugar. Season with salt and pepper and cook until the liquid is slightly reduced, 9 to 10 minutes. Remove the lobster shells and discard. Cut the lobster meat into ½-inch pieces and stir into the sauce. Cook 2 minutes longer until the lobster has become opaque.

2. Meanwhile, in a large saucepot over high heat, bring 4 quarts water to boiling. Add salt to taste and the spaghetti. Cook until al dente, 7 to 9 minutes. Drain well and transfer to serving dishes. Spoon sauce over the spaghetti and serve immediately, garnished with basil.

VARIATION

Pasta with Crab Sauce
Substitute ½ pound fresh or thawed frozen crabmeat that has been picked over and any shell pieces removed. Stir into the sauce and remove pan from the heat. Spoon sauce over spaghetti and serve.

Linguine with Zucchini and Blue Cheese

Use a vegetable peeler to slice the zucchini into long ribbons.

PREP TIME: 5 MINUTES • COOK TIME: 5 MINUTES • MAKES: 4 SERVINGS

Salt
9 ounces fresh linguine
6 tablespoons unsalted butter
1 tablespoon minced garlic
1 medium zucchini, thinly sliced lengthwise
½ cup blue cheese crumbles
Freshly ground black pepper
½ cup grated Parmesan cheese, plus more
    for serving

1. In a large saucepot over high heat, bring 2 quarts water to boiling. Add salt to taste and the linguine. Cook until al dente, 3 to 4 minutes. Drain well.

2. Meanwhile, in a medium skillet over medium-high heat, melt the butter. Add the garlic and cook 1 minute. Stir in the zucchini and the blue cheese.

3. Add the linguine to the skillet. Toss with the sauce until some of the sauce is absorbed, about 1 minute. Sprinkle with salt, pepper, and ½ cup Parmesan and toss until mixed. Serve immediately with additional Parmesan on the side.

VARIATION

Provençal Linguine with Zucchini and Blue Cheese
Add ½ teaspoon dried herbes de Provence to the zucchini. Continue as directed above.

Linguine with Mussels, Tomatoes, and Saffron

If you're not a fan of mussels, substitute 3 pounds of small clams instead.

PREP TIME: 15 MINUTES • COOK TIME: 25 MINUTES • MAKES: 4 SERVINGS

3 tablespoons extra-virgin olive oil

2 ribs celery, thinly sliced

1 small red onion, cut in half and thinly
   sliced

½ teaspoon fennel seed

Large pinch saffron threads

⅓ cup sweet white wine (such as Riesling)

1 cup diced canned Italian tomatoes

¼ cup heavy cream

3 pounds mussels, scrubbed
   and debearded

Salt and freshly ground
   black pepper

1 pound linguine

1. In a large saucepot over medium-high heat, heat the oil. Add the celery, onion, and fennel seed. Cook, stirring occasionally, until celery and onion are soft, about 8 minutes. Stir in the saffron, wine, tomatoes, and cream and bring to simmering. Stir in the mussels. Cover and cook, stirring occasionally, until the mussels open, 5 to 7 minutes. Season with salt and pepper. Using a slotted spoon, transfer the mussels to a plate, discarding any that have not opened. Simmer liquid until reduced by half (to about 2 cups), 2 to 3 minutes.

2. Meanwhile, in a large saucepot over high heat, bring 4 quarts water to boiling. Add salt to taste and the linguine. Cook until al dente, 6 to 8 minutes. Drain well and transfer to a large serving dish. Spoon the mussels and sauce over the linguine and toss until mixed. Serve immediately.

Linguine with Mixed Seafood

Before cooking, be sure to go through the mussels and discard any with broken shells and any that don't close when you tap on them.

PREP TIME: 10 MINUTES • COOK TIME: 35 MINUTES • MAKES: 4 SERVINGS

¼ cup extra-virgin olive oil
Pinch red pepper flakes
4 cloves garlic, peeled and crushed lightly
1 can (28 ounces) diced tomatoes, with
   their juices
1 can (6.5 ounces) chopped clams
1 teaspoon sugar
Salt and freshly ground black pepper
1 pound fresh mussels, scrubbed and
   debearded
½ pound shelled and deveined large shrimp
1 pound spaghetti
2 tablespoons chopped parsley, for garnish
Grated Parmesan cheese, for
   serving

1. In a large skillet over medium-high heat, heat the olive oil. Add the pepper flakes and garlic and cook until garlic is golden, about 2 minutes. Stir in the tomatoes, clams, and sugar. Season with salt and pepper. Simmer 20 minutes, until liquid is quite reduced and thick. Stir in the mussels and cover. Cook until they open, about 5 minutes. Stir in the shrimp and cook 2 minutes. Cover and let stand 5 minutes. Taste for seasoning and add additional salt and pepper if desired. Discard any mussels that haven't opened. Remove the garlic cloves, if desired.

2. Meanwhile, in a large saucepot over high heat, bring 4 quarts water to boiling. Add salt to taste and the spaghetti. Cook until al dente, 7 to 9 minutes. Drain and return to the saucepot. Pour the seafood mixture over the spaghetti and toss until mixed. Transfer to a serving dish, sprinkle with the parsley, and serve. Serve with Parmesan on the side.

Herbed Lamb Steaks with Creamy Pesto Linguine

Substitute eight ¾-inch-thick rib lamb chops for a special occasion (the broiling time is the same). If you use finely ground salt and pepper, use only ½ teaspoon each in the herb mixture for the lamb.

PREP TIME: 10 MINUTES • COOK TIME: 10 MINUTES • MAKES: 4 SERVINGS

2 tablespoons minced garlic

2 tablespoons crumbled dried herbes de Provence

2 tablespoons extra-virgin olive oil

Coarse salt and freshly ground black pepper

4 leg lamb steaks (¾ inch thick, about ½ pound each)

12 ounces linguine

⅓ cup pesto

3 tablespoons crème fraîche

Grated Parmesan cheese

1. Heat the broiler. Line a broiler pan or jelly-roll pan with foil. In a small bowl, stir together the garlic, herbes de Provence, olive oil, and 1 teaspoon each coarse salt and pepper. Spread mixture evenly on the steaks. Broil 1 inch from the heat until nicely browned, 2 to 3 minutes. Turn the steaks and broil 2 to 4 minutes longer for medium-rare.

2. Meanwhile, in a large saucepot over high heat, bring 3 quarts water to boiling. Add salt to taste and the linguine. Cook until al dente, 6 to 9 minutes. Drain and return to the saucepot. Add the pesto, crème fraîche, and ½ cup Parmesan and toss until mixed. Season with salt and pepper, toss again, and divide among serving dishes. Top each serving with a lamb steak and serve immediately.

Rigatoni with Chicken, Onions, and Olives

Here's a perfect dish for using up leftover roast chicken or a deli-roasted chicken from the supermarket.

PREP TIME: 10 MINUTES • COOK TIME: 20 MINUTES • MAKES: 4 SERVINGS

¼ cup extra-virgin olive oil
1 large yellow onion, cut in half and
   thinly sliced
¼ teaspoon sugar
Salt and freshly ground black pepper
2 cups shredded roast chicken
⅓ cup pitted Kalamata olives, chopped
2 tablespoons chopped Italian parsley
12 ounces rigatoni
Grated Asiago cheese, for serving

1. In a large skillet over medium heat, heat the oil. Add the onion and sprinkle with the sugar, salt, and pepper. Cook until very soft and sweet but not brown, about 15 minutes. Stir in the chicken, olives, and parsley, and cook until warmed through, about 2 minutes.

2. Meanwhile, in a large saucepot over high heat, bring 3 quarts water to boiling. Add salt to taste and the rigatoni. Cook until al dente, 7 to 9 minutes. Drain well and transfer to a large serving dish. Spoon the sauce over the rigatoni and toss until mixed. Serve with grated cheese on the side.

Rigatoni with Tomatoes, Red Wine, and Sausage

Here's a chance to experiment with different flavors of chicken sausage, such as basil and sun-dried tomato or garlic and herb.

PREP TIME: 5 MINUTES • COOK TIME: 30 MINUTES • MAKES: 4 SERVINGS

2 tablespoons extra-virgin olive oil
4 chicken sausages (about 1 pound)
1 tablespoon minced garlic
Pinch red pepper flakes
½ cup red wine
1 jar (25 ounces) tomato pasta sauce
Salt and freshly ground black pepper
¼ teaspoon dried rosemary
1 pound rigatoni
Grated Parmesan cheese, for serving

1. In a large skillet over medium-high heat, heat the oil. Add the sausages and cook until browned on most sides, 6 to 7 minutes. Transfer to a plate.

2. Add the garlic and pepper flakes to the skillet and cook 30 seconds. Add the wine and scrape up any browned bits up from the bottom. Simmer until reduced by half, about 3 minutes. Stir in the sauce, add ½ cup water to the jar, swish it around, and add the water to the skillet. Season with salt and pepper, add the rosemary, and return the sausages to the skillet. Simmer until sausages are cooked through, 12 to 14 minutes.

3. Meanwhile, in a large saucepot over high heat, bring 2 quarts water to boiling. Add salt to taste and the rigatoni. Cook until al dente, 6 to 9 minutes. Drain and transfer back to the saucepot. Pour the sauce over and toss until mixed. Divide rigatoni among serving dishes, top each with a sausage, and serve with Parmesan on the side.

Spaghetti with Mushroom Tapenade

Refrigerated tapenade has the freshest flavor. If it's not available, use a shelf-stable jarred version.

PREP TIME: 5 MINUTES • COOK TIME: 20 MINUTES • MAKES: 4 SERVINGS

Salt
1 pound spaghetti
4 tablespoons extra-virgin olive oil
½ cup minced shallots (2 large)
1 package (8 ounces) sliced cremini or
    button mushrooms
Freshly ground black pepper
1 container (4.8 ounces) tapenade
2 tablespoons chopped Italian parsley
Grated pecorino Romano cheese,
    for serving

1. In a large saucepot over high heat, bring 4 quarts water to boiling. Add salt to taste and the spaghetti. Cook until al dente, 7 to 9 minutes. Drain and transfer to a serving bowl.

2. Meanwhile, in a large skillet over high heat, heat the oil. Add the shallots and cook until soft, 3 to 4 minutes. Add the mushrooms and sprinkle with salt and pepper. Cook until tender and browned, about 8 minutes. Add the tapenade mixture, parsley, and mushrooms to the spaghetti and toss until mixed. Serve with grated cheese on the side.

Farfalle with Balsamic Mushroom Sauce

If you have a 12-inch skillet, use it here. If you don't have one, add as many mushrooms as you can fit and add more once they cook down.

PREP TIME: 5 MINUTES • COOK TIME: 15 MINUTES • MAKES: 4 SERVINGS

Salt

1 pound farfalle

3 tablespoons extra-virgin olive oil

3 packages (8 ounces each) sliced cremini mushrooms

1 tablespoon minced garlic

½ teaspoon dried thyme

Freshly ground black pepper

2 tablespoons balsamic vinegar

⅓ cup heavy cream

Grated Parmesan cheese, for serving

1. In a large saucepot over high heat, bring 4 quarts water to boiling. Add salt to taste and the farfalle. Cook until al dente, 6 to 9 minutes. Drain well and transfer to a large serving dish.

2. Meanwhile, in a large skillet over high heat, heat the oil. Add the mushrooms and cook without stirring until mushrooms are browned on the bottom, 3 to 4 minutes. Stir and cook until the mushrooms are tender, 3 to 4 minutes longer. Add the garlic and thyme, season with salt and pepper, and cook 1 minute longer. Stir in the vinegar and cream and bring to simmering. Spoon the sauce over the farfalle and toss to mix. Serve with Parmesan on the side.

Fettuccine with Vodka Sauce

To complete this meal, simply add a Caesar salad and warm bread.

PREP TIME: 5 MINUTES • COOK TIME: 15 MINUTES • MAKES: 4 SERVINGS

1 can (28 ounces) Italian plum tomatoes
¼ cup extra-virgin olive oil
2 tablespoons finely chopped garlic
¼ teaspoon red pepper flakes
⅓ cup vodka
Salt and freshly ground black pepper
⅓ cup heavy cream
1 pound fettuccine
Fresh basil leaves, torn, for garnish
Grated Parmesan cheese, for serving

1. Pour the tomatoes and their liquid into a food processor and process until smooth. Set aside.

2. In a large skillet, heat the olive oil until very hot but not smoking. Add the garlic and pepper flakes to the pan and cook until the garlic is golden, about 1 minute. Add the tomatoes and vodka. Bring to boiling, season with salt and pepper, and reduce the heat to medium-low. Simmer, uncovered, about 8 minutes and add the cream. Simmer 3 to 4 minutes longer and season with salt and pepper.

3. In a large saucepot over high heat, bring 2 quarts water to boiling. Add salt to taste and the fettuccine. Cook until al dente, 6 to 8 minutes. Drain well and transfer to a large serving bowl. Pour the sauce over, toss, and sprinkle with torn basil leaves. Serve with Parmesan on the side.

VARIATION

Fettuccine and Shrimp with Vodka Sauce
Sauté 1 pound large peeled and deveined shrimp in the oil until just pink, tossing constantly, 1 to 2 minutes. Remove the shrimp to a plate with a slotted spoon and continue with the garlic as above. Stir the shrimp back into the sauce after it has been simmered with the cream.

Straw and Hay Fettucine

This very pretty dish would be perfect for brunch.

PREP TIME: 10 MINUTES • COOK TIME: 12 MINUTES • MAKES: 4 SERVINGS

½ stick (¼ cup) unsalted butter
1 package (8 ounces) sliced white
   mushrooms
Salt and freshly ground black pepper
1 cup heavy cream
½ cup diced ham
½ cup frozen baby peas
¼ teaspoon grated nutmeg
8 ounces fresh spinach fettuccine
8 ounces fresh plain fettuccine
1 cup (about 2 ounces) packed coarsely
   chopped washed arugula
½ cup grated Parmesan cheese, plus more
   for serving

1. In a large skillet over medium-high heat, melt the butter. Add the mushrooms, salt, and pepper and cook, stirring, until tender, about 5 minutes. Pour in the cream, bring to simmering and cook until lightly reduced, about 3 minutes. Stir in the ham, peas, and nutmeg and season with salt and pepper. Remove from heat and set aside.

2. In a large saucepot over high heat, bring 4 quarts water to boiling. Add salt to taste and both pastas. Cook until al dente, 3 to 4 minutes. Drain well and transfer to a large serving bowl. Throw in the arugula, pour the mushroom mixture over, and toss. Sprinkle with Parmesan and serve immediately with additional cheese on the side.

Butter and Parmesan Fettuccine

To soften the butter, put it in the microwave on high power for 10 seconds.

PREP TIME: 5 MINUTES • COOKING TIME: 4 MINUTES • MAKES: 4 SERVINGS

1 stick (½ cup) unsalted butter, cut into
   6 pieces, at room temperature
1 cup grated Parmesan cheese
Salt
1 pound fresh fettuccine
Freshly ground black pepper

1. Place the butter and Parmesan in a large serving bowl. Set aside without mixing.

2. In a large saucepot over high heat, bring 4 quarts water to boiling. Add salt to taste and the fettuccine. Cook until al dente, 3 to 4 minutes. Drain and pour the fettuccine on top of the cheese mixture. Toss until mixed and butter is melted. Season with salt and pepper and serve.

Parmesan and Mint Alfredo

You could also add sautéed zucchini or steamed baby peas to this super-easy Alfredo. I like a generous amount of black pepper—feel free to adjust the amount you use to your taste.

PREP TIME: 5 MINUTES • COOK TIME: 9 MINUTES • MAKES: 4 SERVINGS

2 tablespoons unsalted butter, cut into
    small pieces
2 large eggs, beaten
1 cup grated Parmesan cheese
½ cup heavy cream
Salt
1 pound ziti
¼ cup chopped fresh mint
Freshly ground black pepper

1. In a large serving bowl, combine the butter, eggs, Parmesan, and cream. Mix lightly and set aside.

2. In a large saucepot over high heat, bring 2 quarts water to boiling. Add salt to taste and the ziti. Cook until al dente, 6 to 9 minutes. Drain the ziti and pour it into the bowl. Add the mint and toss lightly. Season with salt and pepper, toss again, and serve.

VARIATION

Parmesan and Basil Alfredo
Omit the mint and substitute ¼ cup roughly torn basil leaves. Prepare as directed above.

Fettuccine with Spinach, Cream, and Pine Nuts

Prewashed baby spinach is a great ingredient to cook with, because it wilts quickly without giving off lots of liquid. I always keep some on hand for salads or easy dishes like this one.

PREP TIME: 5 MINUTES • **COOK TIME: 7 MINUTES** • **MAKES: 4 SERVINGS**

¼ cup pine nuts, for garnish
½ stick (¼ cup) unsalted butter
1 tablespoon minced garlic
¼ teaspoon red pepper flakes
6 ounces washed baby spinach
½ cup heavy cream
Salt and freshly ground black pepper
¼ teaspoon freshly grated nutmeg
12 ounces fresh fettuccine
Grated Parmesan cheese, for serving

1. In a large skillet over medium-high heat, toss the pine nuts until lightly toasted, 2 to 3 minutes. Transfer to a bowl. In the same skillet over medium-high heat, melt the butter. Add the garlic and pepper flakes and cook 1 minute. Add the spinach and stir until it starts to wilt. Add the cream and bring to simmering. Season with salt, pepper, and the nutmeg, remove from the heat, and set aside.

2. In a large saucepot over high heat, bring 3 quarts water to boiling. Add salt to taste and the fettuccine. Cook until al dente, 3 to 4 minutes. Drain well and transfer to the skillet. Toss, simmering, until some of the sauce is absorbed, 1 to 2 minutes. Transfer to a serving bowl, sprinkle with the pine nuts, and serve with Parmesan on the side.

Smoked Turkey Tetrazzini

Traditionally, this dish is baked in a casserole. This version omits the baking step, but is just as tasty as the original. Have your supermarket deli cut half-inch slices of smoked turkey for you to dice into cubes.

PREP TIME: 5 MINUTES • **COOK TIME: 12 MINUTES** • **MAKES: 4 SERVINGS**

Salt
12 ounces fettuccine
¼ cup slivered almonds
½ stick (¼ cup) unsalted butter
1 package (8 ounces) sliced white
  mushrooms
Freshly ground black pepper
1 cup heavy cream
¼ teaspoon freshly grated nutmeg
2 cups diced smoked turkey
1 tablespoon lemon juice
3 tablespoons grated Parmesan cheese,
  plus more for serving

1. In a large saucepot over high heat, bring 3 quarts water to boiling. Add salt to taste and the fettuccine. Cook until al dente, 6 to 9 minutes. Drain well.

2. Meanwhile, in a large skillet over medium-high heat, cook the almonds, tossing them until they are lightly toasted, 2 to 3 minutes. Transfer to a bowl. In the same skillet, melt the butter. Add the mushrooms and sprinkle with salt and pepper. Cook, stirring, until tender, about 5 minutes. Add the cream and bring to simmering. Simmer until the liquid is slightly reduced, about 3 minutes. Stir in the nutmeg and turkey.

3. Transfer the pasta to the skillet. Add the lemon juice and toss until the noodles absorb some of the sauce, 1 to 2 minutes. Transfer to a serving bowl, sprinkle with the almonds, and 3 tablespoons Parmesan. Serve with additional cheese on the side.

Fettucine with Tomatoes and Chicken Livers

This pasta is strictly for chicken liver lovers.

PREP TIME: 10 MINUTES • **COOK TIME: 15 MINUTES** • **MAKES: 4 SERVINGS**

2 tablespoons extra-virgin olive oil

1 tablespoon minced garlic

Pinch red pepper flakes

½ pound chicken livers, trimmed of fat
   and connective tissue

Salt and freshly ground black pepper

1 can (28 ounces) crushed Italian
   tomatoes

¼ teaspoon dried sage

1 teaspoon sugar

1 tablespoon chopped Italian parsley

1 pound fettucine

Grated Parmesan cheese, for serving

1. In a large skillet over medium-high heat, heat the oil. Add the garlic, pepper flakes, and livers and sprinkle with salt and pepper. Cook until the livers are browned on the outside but still pink on the inside, about 2 minutes. Transfer to a plate and pour the tomatoes into the skillet. Stir in the sage and sugar, season with salt and pepper, and simmer until thickened, about 5 minutes. Coarsely chop the livers and return them to the skillet. Stir in the parsley.

2. In a large saucepot over high heat, bring 4 quarts water to boiling. Add salt to taste and the fettuccine. Cook until al dente, 6 to 9 minutes. Drain and transfer back to the saucepot. Pour the sauce over and toss. Serve with grated cheese.

Spinach and Prosciutto Fettuccine

Steam some green beans or make a simple green salad while you're cooking the pasta. Add a loaf of crusty bread, and you've got a wonderful meal.

PREP TIME: 10 MINUTES • **COOK TIME: 4 MINUTES** • **MAKES: 4 SERVINGS**

4 cups (packed) washed baby spinach
2 ounces prosciutto, chopped (about
 ½ cup)
1 stick (½ cup) unsalted butter, softened
 and cut into 6 pieces
1 cup grated Parmesan cheese
Salt
1 pound fettuccine
Freshly ground black pepper

1. Place the spinach, prosciutto, butter, and Parmesan in a large serving bowl. Set aside without mixing.

2. In a large saucepot over high heat, bring 4 quarts water to boiling. Add salt to taste and the fettuccine. Cook until al dente, 6 to 9 minutes. Drain, pour the fettuccine over the spinach mixture, and toss until mixed. Season with salt and pepper and serve.

Fettuccine with Artichokes and Crab

Here are the flavors of everyone's favorite dip, transformed into a pasta dish. Season it with lots of freshly ground black pepper.

PREP TIME: 10 MINUTES • COOK TIME: 10 MINUTES • MAKES: 4 SERVINGS

Salt
1 pound fettuccine
2 tablespoons unsalted butter
½ cup finely chopped shallots
1 can (13.75 ounces) artichoke hearts, drained and coarsely chopped
½ cup heavy cream
½ cup sour cream
1 tablespoon chopped fresh tarragon
1 can (6 ounces) crabmeat, drained
Freshly ground black pepper
Grated Parmesan cheese, for serving

1. In a large saucepot over high heat, bring 4 quarts water to boiling. Add salt to taste and the fettuccine. Cook until al dente, 7 to 9 minutes. Drain well and transfer to a large serving dish.

2. Meanwhile, in a large skillet over medium-high heat, melt the butter. Cook the shallots until softened, 3 to 4 minutes. Stir in the artichoke hearts, cream, and sour cream. Bring to simmering. Stir in the tarragon and crab. Season with salt and pepper. Spoon sauce over the fettuccine and toss until mixed. Serve with cheese and additional black pepper on the side.

Fettuccine with Smoked Salmon

This tremendously rich dish, served in smaller portions, is perfect as a first course for six.

PREP TIME: 10 MINUTES • COOK TIME: 15 MINUTES • MAKES: 4 SERVINGS

Salt

9 ounces fresh fettuccine

3 tablespoons lemon-flavored olive or avocado oil

2 shallots, finely chopped

1/8 teaspoon red pepper flakes

1/2 cup heavy cream

3/4 cup chicken broth

Zest of 1 lemon

Freshly ground black pepper

2 ounces smoked salmon (lox style), cut into thin strips

1 tablespoon snipped chives

1. In a large saucepot over high heat, bring 2 quarts water to boiling. Add salt to taste and the fettucine. Cook until almost al dente, 3 to 4 minutes. Drain.

2. Meanwhile, in a medium skillet over medium-high heat, heat the oil. Add the shallots and pepper flakes and cook until shallots are soft, 3 to 4 minutes. Add the cream, broth, and zest and bring to simmering. Simmer until broth has reduced slightly, about 3 minutes. Season with salt and pepper Add the cooked fettuccine to the skillet. Over medium heat, toss the fettuccine and the sauce until the sauce is absorbed, 1 to 2 minutes. Add the salmon and chives and toss again until mixed. Serve immediately.

Scallops with Sun-Dried Tomato Sauce

This pasta combines intense Mediterranean-style flavors with the mild flavor of sea scallops.

PREP TIME: 10 MINUTES • COOK TIME: 10 MINUTES • MAKES: 4 SERVINGS

Salt
9 ounces fresh fettuccine
1 stick unsalted butter, cut in half
1 pound fresh sea scallops (cut in half horizontally if large)
Freshly ground black pepper
1 tablespoon minced garlic
Pinch red pepper flakes
¼ cup jarred sun-dried tomatoes in oil, cut into thin strips
Finely grated zest of 1 orange
2 tablespoons chopped Italian parsley
1 teaspoon chopped fresh thyme

1. In a large saucepot over high heat, bring 2 quarts water to boiling. Add salt to taste and the fettuccine. Cook until al dente, 3 to 4 minutes. Drain well.

2. Meanwhile, in a large skillet over high heat, melt half the butter. Add the scallops and sprinkle with salt and pepper. Cook just until the scallops are opaque, 2 to 3 minutes total. Transfer to a plate and cover with foil to keep warm. Add the remaining butter to the skillet. Add the garlic, pepper flakes, sun-dried tomatoes, orange zest, parsley, and thyme and cook 2 minutes. Season with salt and pepper. Transfer fettuccine to the skillet. Toss to mix and divide the fettuccine among serving dishes. Arrange scallops on top of each serving and serve immediately.

Gnocchi with Walnut Sauce

Since gnocchi tend to be rich, serve something light like a mixed green salad or steamed broccoli as a side dish. This dish is also a lovely first course for six—just serve slightly smaller portions.

PREP TIME: 5 MINUTES • COOK TIME: 5 MINUTES • MAKES: 4 SERVINGS

Salt
1 package (1 pound 1 ounce) fresh gnocchi
½ stick (¼ cup) unsalted butter
1 tablespoon finely chopped garlic
½ cup coarsely chopped walnuts
¼ cup heavy cream
Freshly ground black pepper
¼ cup grated Parmesan cheese, plus more
    for serving
16 fresh basil leaves, torn, for garnish

1. In a large saucepot over high heat, bring 4 quarts water to boiling. Add salt to taste and the gnocchi. Cook until the gnocchi float to the top, 2 to 3 minutes. Drain well and transfer to a large serving bowl.

2. Meanwhile, in a medium skillet over medium-high heat, melt the butter. Add the garlic and walnuts and stir until the garlic is golden, about 1 minute. Stir in the cream and bring to simmering. Season with salt and pepper. Pour the sauce over the gnocchi, sprinkle with ¼ cup Parmesan and basil, and toss until mixed. Serve with additional Parmesan on the side.

VARIATION

Gnocchi with Blue Cheese and Walnuts
Prepare as directed above. Add ¼ cup crumbled blue cheese to the gnocchi when tossing with the Parmesan and basil.

Gnocchi with Leeks and Peas

This dish tastes like springtime. Be sure to wash the leek very thoroughly.

PREP TIME: 5 MINUTES • COOK TIME: 10 MINUTES • MAKES: 4 SERVINGS

1 stick (½ cup) unsalted butter
1 tablespoon finely chopped garlic
1 large leek (white and tender green),
    washed and chopped
½ cup frozen baby peas
Salt and freshly ground black pepper
1 package (1 pound 1 ounce) fresh gnocchi
¼ cup grated Parmesan cheese, plus more
    for serving
1 tablespoon snipped chives, for garnish

1. In a medium skillet over medium-high heat, melt the butter. Add the garlic and leek and cook, stirring frequently, until the leek is soft, 3 to 4 minutes. Stir in the peas and simmer 2 minutes. Season with salt and pepper.

2. Meanwhile, in a large saucepot over high heat, bring 4 quarts water to boiling. Add salt to taste and the gnocchi. Cook until the gnocchi float to the top, 2 to 3 minutes. Drain well and transfer to a serving bowl. Pour sauce over the gnocchi, sprinkle with ¼ cup Parmesan, and toss until mixed. Sprinkle with chives. Serve with additional Parmesan on the side.

VARIATION

Gnocchi with Leeks, Peas, and Ham
Stir in ½ cup diced Black Forest ham when you add the peas to the skillet.

170

1 7 1

176

178